Exit 12

Martin McGregor

Exit 12. A novel by Martin McGregor

First published in the UK in 2018, by Marlebond Publishing Ltd. Second edition 2020.

ISBN: 9781982926076

Original cover design by Tama66 on Pixabay

Also, by the author:

Ellie Caitlin the complete collection

Keep away from the windows

Keep away from the windows 2: The dark ones

Keep away from the windows 3: The world in my eyes

Damaged Goods

24

24: The return

Introduction

For those of you, who are not familiar with road numbers, the exit 12 used in the title of this book, is located on the M25. This exit or junction if you prefer, leads to the M3, which then, in turn, leads to the A303 and ultimately this road leads back to my home. The idea for this book came as I was sitting in front of the television watching a trailer for a new horror movie that was now playing at the cinema.

The narrator was talking in a deep voice, and he was describing the depths of the scares that were to be found within the movie. I tried to think of a title, of something that would sound as dramatic if it were also being described in such a trailer.

I had recently taken a few car journeys on the M25, and it really can be a God awful road at times (as anyone who has ever driven on it around five in the afternoon on a weekday would probably attest to). On our latest trip, we had encountered long delays whilst on the return journey. I was fed up and frustrated at the slow pace. I was desperate to reach exit 12. That junction is still about an hour's drive away from my home, but I always feel a sense of relief when I finally reach it. It somehow makes it seem like I am almost home.

This is how the title for this novel was born. Now that I had a title, all that I needed were some ideas as to how the story would unfold. The initial idea for the story came from an unusual source of inspiration, and that was from avoiding the numerous potholes that I encounter whilst driving around Andover daily. Upon reading this story, you will no doubt see where this fits in. Then the story began to take a much darker turn for me.

Within every story ever written, I believe that there are always elements of truth and that authors will look at personal experiences from the past to fuel their creative fires. I had to draw on my own experiences from the past to enable me to complete this book. Writing this book touched me in ways that I could have never expected. I will say no more about this, and I will leave you to read the book for yourself without revealing any further details to you. I will leave you to consider which parts of the book relate to me personally, but I will probably never divulge this information.

A lyric from one of my favourite songs, states that 'The past is another country'. Those are very wise words, indeed. The past is something that is forever gone but that we can never really leave behind. Each of us has made mistakes in life, and each of us carries with us some form of regret. All of us will look back at some point in our lives and say 'what if I had done this instead?'

All of us will also reach a point of finality in our lives where we can no longer reflect on the past. We can no longer make amends for the errors of our ways, or to change the way that others see us. One day it will just be too late for that. When we draw our final breath, only then will we know the truth of our existence. We will never know if we will be remembered or consigned to history along with billions who have gone before us. Most of us will be forgotten with the sands of time.

I also decided to do something that I have never done before, and I included a few surprises inside of this book where readers of my previous novels might be able to relate. I was expanding my literary universe as it were to include characters who are already known by my fans, and that has only added to my enjoyment.

I honestly hope that you enjoy this book if you do, then please tell your friends about it. If you don't enjoy it, then please tell me. I can only grow as a writer if I learn from my mistakes, and slowly I feel as if I am getting there. Today, I am going to enjoy some glorious April sunshine before I start to ponder my next project.

2018 looks set to be a busy year for me, and I hope that you come along and enjoy the ride as well. Wishing you all a fantastic summer

Martin McGregor April 2018

Thank you to my four sons, Nick, Chris, Jordan, Owen. To Tonya, Emma, Michelle and a special thank you to Jo Renfrey and Heather Swinson for all of your help. Lastly to every one of you who keep believing in me. I hope that this book repays your faith in some small way.

For Atlanta Rain

Love Dad

The business meeting had gone far better than anyone could have expected, and it had been judged to be a complete and utter success. Months of hard work, of planning and of those laborious hours spent travelling up and down those cursed motorways, could now finally come to an end. The merger talks had been completed, and all orders the paperwork had been signed off as well.

The amalgamation of the two companies would go ahead in November of this year. It would mean that he would have to relocate, but the new parent company were more than happy to pay all his moving expenses in return for the expertise that he was able to bring to the table.

His calculations and presentations had convinced them that the amount that he would save the company with this new merger was phenomenal. Alan welcomed the new challenges that lay ahead of him. He was already a board member, but his aspirations didn't end there. He wanted to reach the very top of his game, and this job was his life. He had never settled down; instead, he preferred to enjoy the perks of short term relationships. It was much easier to live life without the complications of having a long term partner presented.

The only downside to the merger was that he was going to have to let some good people go. They were just collateral damage in the grander scheme of things. It wasn't the first time that he had been forced to axe staff, and it wouldn't be the last time either. It was nothing personal, of course; it was purely a business decision. Letting them go this close to Christmas would mean that most of them would be able to find some other work, even if it was only in temporary positions. He was sure that they would all get by in the end. That wasn't his problem, though.

He began the drive through the Dartford tunnel, and if it weren't for the solid double lines painted through the middle of the road in the tunnel, then he would have overtaken the slowcoach who was now driving far too slowly in front of him. The driver was driving at least ten miles below the speed limit, and Alan was desperate to get home before it got too late in the evening. The M25 could be a nightmare at this time of night, but so far it had been flowing quite freely, which was much to his surprise.

When he came out on the other side of the tunnel, he started to apply more pressure to the accelerator. Now that he was out on the open road, he drifted into the outer lane, and he overtook the slow-moving idiot, who looked as if she could only just about see over the steering wheel. He shook his head to show her his disapproval of her poor driving skills as he sped past her. There were just too many Sunday drivers on the roads these days.

Then without any prior warning, the skies suddenly decided to open up above him, and heavy rain began to fall. He activated the windscreen wipers to clear his view, but it was raining far heavier when he reached the junction for the M-three. He indicated quite late and then he turned off at exit twelve. He would remain on this motorway until he reached the A-three o three which was the road that would take him home to Andover.

The weather in this country was very unpredictable these days, and being March, the sudden switch between brilliant sunshine to sudden downpours was almost becoming standard in Britain for this time of year. Rain hammered downward in fierce torrents that splattered against the windscreen, and it obscured his vision almost completely.

He hated driving in the rain with a passion. The wipers were already on the fastest setting, but they were fighting a losing battle against the weather when it was this extreme. The front tyre of his car then struck a deep pothole in the road, that he could not have possibly seen.

The suspension of the car viciously juddered as he struck yet another unseen pothole further along the road. Alan cursed his stupidity. The wipers were having a hypnotic effect on him, and he had just been starting to doze off at the wheel. The jarring on the steering wheel had shaken him awake again with a frightening dose of reality. He had fallen asleep at the wheel before. He had done it more than once as well.

There was something about long-distance driving that always made him feel a little too relaxed while he was in the driver's seat. It was only through pure luck that he hadn't sideswiped another car, or even worse, he might have drifted over into the outside lane and crashed into the central reservation. Now there was an annoying knocking sound now coming from what sounded like the front wheel axle of the car. There was a judgement call that he alone would now have to make.

It was a risk that could prove very costly if he got it wrong. He could pull over onto the hard shoulder (and that would mean standing outside of the car in the pouring rain while he waited for a tow-truck), or he could take a chance and try to continue driving with a damaged car until he reached the next junction. He decided that the exit was close enough for him to head for the turn and to risk driving those few extra miles.

When he reached the turn that laid on to the A303, then he could find the safety of a lay-by or perhaps even a side road for him to park up. The exit was signposted up ahead. The turn off to the A303 was only one mile away. He had already decided that he was going to go for it. He kept his fingers crossed that the knocking sound wouldn't get any worse.

He kept on going until the green marker signs descended from three to one hundred yards, and then he indicated in advance of taking the turn off. It was just gone eight o'clock in the evening, and the light was already fading. It would have been dark already by now if it wasn't for the recent clock changes to keep the countries farmers in line with the daylight saving time adjustments.

Then there was another judder, and the banging sound that was coming from underneath the car started getting louder by the second. He turned off on to the slip road that took him off the motorway, but he was still about a twenty-minute drive away from his house.

He had driven this road a vast number of times without ever paying it a great deal of attention. He was pretty certain that there was a lay-by not far away from where he currently was. He was sure that he had seen police speed traps set up on that stretch of road before. Those traps were just another way to milk drivers of more money, and they infuriated him. He believed that the speed limits here should be the same as in Germany on the autobahns. That would get things moving for business travellers and the industry as a whole.

The windscreen wipers continued to battle relentlessly against the rain, which now seemed to be falling even heavier than before if that was even possible. The banging sound underneath the car made the wheels judder slightly, and the combination of both the noise and the jolting motion seemed to have a hypnotic effect on him. He was trying to fight the feeling of his eyes becoming heavy, and his desire to sleep.

He was trying so hard to stay awake, but he felt his eyelids start to close anyway. He had to do more to fight off the tiredness, so he opened up the car window just a small amount to allow some fresh air to come inside of the car. The rain found its way in through even the tiniest of openings, and it sprayed up into his face. He could now see that he was right about a lay-by; it was just up ahead. He pushed up the indicator lever and made ready to pull the car into the safety of the gap.

Alan entered the lay-by, and he slowed the car down until it came to a full stop. He then pulled up the handbrake lever until it was fully engaged and then he dipped the clutch, nudging the gearstick forwards into the first gear position as well. Safety first, he said to himself. It was an old habit that he had picked up from when he used to have to park on a driveway on a steep hill. Now he could not stop himself from doing it if he tried.

He pressed the dashboard button that activated the hazard lights, and then he sat with his eyes closed for a few moments. He had hoped that it might help to lift this feeling of exhaustion. It was making no difference, though. Now that the car was parked up, he was no longer feeling sleepy. The rain seemed to have eased a little, so he stepped out of the door to see if he could spot the damage that had been caused when the wheel had struck that damned pothole.

If there was anything seriously wrong with his car, then he was going to be on the phone complaining about those bloody potholes the minute that the council offices were open in the morning. He paid enough car tax and council tax over the years, not forgetting the excessive tax on petrol as well. The least he and every other driver out there deserved were roads that were fit to drive on. The rain was still coming down lightly, so he turned the collar of his shirt up to try and deflect some of the rain. It didn't help in the slightest. The tiny drops of water still ran down the back of his neck.

He didn't need to examine the car too closely. The issue was visible as the car had two badly damaged tyres. Both of them on the driver's side looked wrecked. This was an emergency call-out repair scenario. If it was just one damaged tyre to deal with, then he could have used the spare wheel that he kept in the boot. He kicked the front wheel hard out of sheer frustration, and he slightly hurt his foot in the process. Cursing his idiocy, he turned around, and then he opened the car door, and he jumped back into the driver's seat.

Alan leaned over to the left and then pulled his mobile phone and wallet out of his right-hand trouser pocket. The battery level on the phone was running a little low. He had left the house at just after five this morning, and it had been a very long day for all involved. The battery level was still showing at eighteen percent, and that was enough to call the breakdown services out and to get his car towed back home.

He opened up his wallet and searched through the numerous business and cash cards that he had collected over the years until he eventually found his breakdown membership card near to the back of them all. "Bingo!" After almost cancelling the service last year, he was now feeling rather pleased with himself that he had kept it running. He turned the card over to find the emergency breakdown number, and then he carefully tapped the number into his phone and pressed the call button.

He had almost cancelled the cover because he had paid for the peace of mind for the last four years, but he had never once used the service at all. He waited for the familiar ringing sound that came when the phone finally connected, but it never happened, only silence from the other end. He tried redialling the number. Then he noticed that the signal strength level was showing at zero. He had probably parked just a little too far away from the nearest telephone antenna.

In frustration, he threw the phone down onto the passenger seat next to him. He threw it so hard that it bounced up ferociously and it connected with the passenger door before finally settling back down on the chair. He noisily made the sound of a vastly exaggerated sigh to an audience of none in his sheer frustration.

He sat in the car while he sulked about his predicament for about fifteen more minutes. In his head, he debated the possibility of spending the night sleeping in the car. He doubted that he would get much sleep if he did that, though. Then the rain started to ease off properly, and it looked as if it was finally going to stop at last.

There was a sign on the edge of the road up ahead, but it was just a little bit too far in the distance for him to be able to read what it said. It was pointing towards something though, so there was another area to explore that was close.

The sign was either pointing towards a local landmark, a village or even better; it could be pointing towards a pub. He could murder a few pints of cold lager right now. Whatever the sign was pointing to, there was a good chance that he might be able to make a phone call from there, or perhaps he could book a room and stay in a hotel for the night.

The thought of a hotel bed was a far better idea than him staying here in the car in the cold all night, so he decided to get out of the car and to take a chance. He picked up his phone from where it had landed on the passenger seat next to him, and then he climbed out of the car. He locked the doors using the remote, and then he began to walk towards the sign on the roadside up ahead of him.

Although the rain had eased off, he was still soaked through to the skin. The rain continued to fall lightly, and he was getting wetter with every minute that passed. It was unavoidable, though. Perhaps should keep an umbrella in the boot of the car in future he suggested to himself? He agreed with the voice in his head that this was a great idea! The rainwater now ran down from his hair, and annoyingly it was getting into his eyes as he walked and it blurred his vision.

He was drawing closer and closer to the sign, but he still couldn't make it out. His eyesight seemed to be getting a little worse with age, and his vanity stopped him from having his eyes tested. The light was fading fast. When he was about thirty feet away from the sign, he could finally make out the words that were written on it.

The sign read 'Grimfall 1 mile' along with a directional arrow that pointed to the left. He had never heard of Grimfall before. It must be a small village he assumed. It was odd as he must have driven past this sign a million times before, and he had never noticed it, not even once. He took a quick look back over his shoulder towards his car, and it was now barely visible in the low light of the evening.

If it wasn't for the hazard lights that were still flashing away repeatedly, then he might not have been able to see the car at all. A one-mile walk was nothing, so he decided to continue. Grimfall might very well have a pub or a restaurant where he could buy something to eat and drink, so it was a no-brainer. His stomach was rumbling, and his mouth was watering while he was thinking about that cold beer again. He turned left and headed off towards Grimfall with a renewed spring in his step.

The first three-quarters of a mile was on a gentle uphill gradient. The roads were uneven and winding as they twisted upward. The wind now started to pick up quite a bit as he walked onward. The cold wind, along with the light rain, was enough to start to send shivers right down his spine. He would appreciate a hot bath or shower right about now.

As he approached yet another blind bend in the road, he suddenly felt a little uncomfortable. It was an odd sensation. It felt like he was being watched by someone or something. Then there was the sudden sound of movement coming from the foliage that was directly over to his right.

Alan took his mobile phone back out from his trouser pocket, and he scrolled to the left as he searched through the multiple screens for the torch app. He found the one that he needed, and he activated it to turn on the light. It was surprisingly powerful for a mobile phone torch, but he knew that it would quickly start to drain away from the power of the phone's battery. He shone the light over toward the trees on his right, but there was nothing to be seen. He rotated it from left to right, and he slowly searched the entire area.

"Hello! Is there anyone out there?" He shouted. He hoped that if any stray animals were hiding in the trees that they might have been scared off upon hearing his voice, but there was no movement, and there was no response. It was only now that Alan realised that he hadn't seen a single car pass him by from the moment that he had pulled into the lay-by, and that was very strange. It was clear that not many people had used this road at all.

If there was someone else in the woods watching him, then they were not in the mood for a conversation. He shone the torch around again slowly in the reverse direction, but he couldn't see anything obvious within the trees. He smiled away to himself as he realised that it must have just been his imagination playing tricks on him. That was what he had to keep telling himself now, that it was just his imagination running wild.

He switched off the torch, and then he checked the battery level on the phone. Despite using the torch for less than a minute, it had now reduced the power level down to just seventeen percent. He just hoped that someone in the village might have a charger that he could borrow. It was a pretty popular phone, so it was quite likely that someone there would have one.

Alan placed the phone safely back in his pocket, and then he continued walking towards Grimfall. From within the trees to his right, there was a low growling sound. The noise stopped him dead in his tracks. There was an animal somewhere within the woods after all, and it sounded as if it was very unfriendly. Alan stood motionless in silence as he watched for any movement in the trees. Within the woods, he was startled as he saw a pair of bright yellow eyes now staring back at him. He gulped down hard on his saliva.

It was an animal all right, and it was a bloody big one too. He had heard numerous stories about wild cats that were roaming free in the

Hampshire countryside. He thought that he had seen one once, but he had simply dismissed the sighting as a trick of the light. Now there was an angry animal that was standing right in front of him, and it was showing no fear of him. That wasn't a good sign.

He now had three choices that were open to him. He could either run towards the animal while making as much noise as he could to try to scare it away, he could stand in place making himself tall and hope that the animal did not see him as a threat (but that was unlikely though). The third option was to run towards Grimfall and pray that he made it to the safety of the village before the animal caught up with him and tried to attack him.

Before he even had the chance to rationalize, what would be the best of the three choices in his head, the fear factor had already made up his mind for him. He had started running towards Grimfall as fast as his legs would carry him. He was heading towards the village at a pace that he hadn’t moved at for a long time, and he wasn't going to stop for anyone or anything until he got there.

The animal was moving through the trees and chasing after him; he could hear it. It was still growling and snarling at him as it ran, and now the noise that it was making was becoming louder and louder. It was running through the woods in parallel with him, but now it sounded as if it were gaining on him. The fear of being caught gave him an added incentive, and he increased his speed even more as he tried to make his escape.

Up ahead of him, Alan could now make out the shape of a large solitary building. Lights were flickering within the ground floor windows, and it looked as if someone was at home. There were no other buildings around there at all, and there were no other houses or shops here either. He could not even see any signs pointing in or out of the village or towards other points of interest. The building was isolated, and it looked as if it had been there for a very long time.

As he ran closer to the perimeter hedges that surrounded the house, he could see a gap in the foliage and the welcoming shape of a doorway arch up ahead of him. Behind, he could hear that the animal's growls and snaps were growing louder by the second. If he stopped to look back, then the animal would probably catch up with him, he was quite sure that it would be a fatal mistake, so he kept his eyes forward. He prayed that he could just make it inside the house before the animal caught him.

Alan now had only one thought that was running through his mind; he was going to run inside of that building and lock the big heavy-looking door behind him. There was just one slight issue that was making him nervous. The success of his entire plan all depended on the door being unlocked so that he could run inside to safety. If it were locked, then he would not have time to wait for someone to come and answer the door to him. He was intent on bursting in unannounced, and then he would apologise for his rudeness once he was safe. He was sure that the occupants would understand, given the dire situation that he now found himself.

His breathing was becoming very heavy and laboured, and he felt a stitch in the side of his stomach. The pain of this impromptu sprinting session seared throughout his chest. He was so out of shape that it was going to take a lot of work to get back to anywhere near to a decent level of fitness. It was only in times like these that showed him that his priorities in life were totally out of sync.

He finally reached the front door, and he pulled the handle downward. Much to his relief, the door opened up without any resistance. He had no time to celebrate the victory just yet though. He burst in through the open door, and he quickly slammed it closed behind him.

As he turned around to close the door, he had

caught just the briefest glimpse of the animal that had been pursuing him through the darkness. It looked like it was a wolf, but the animal was huge. It was nothing like any other wolf he had ever seen on television or in the movies. It had saliva drooling from its fangs as it had anticipated catching its prey. Alan secured the door as he drew the deadbolt over the top of the frame. He was now safe. Well, for the present moment, he was relatively safe anyway.

The entire weight of the animal then crashed into the wooden door, and the wood seemed to bend inwards with the pressure now being forced against it. The animal must have been immensely strong. The impact of the animal charging at the door had shocked Alan so much, that he fell backwards onto the floor beneath him and now he crawled away backwards on his elbows in a state of utter panic.

The animal then rammed itself against the door again, and for a split second, Alan feared that the door might give way under the repeated pressure. He kept moving backwards on his elbows, now using his feet as well to help him crawl back as far away from the door as he could get. The animal seemed determined to get inside the house, no matter what.

Alan breathed much more heavily, and as he moved backwards, his lungs felt like they were on fire. He yelped out in childlike fright as his head struck something wooden behind him. He could go back no further. He looked upward to see that he was now pressed up against a counter of some kind. He focussed on the door in front of him, fully expecting it to give way any second. His eyes were now wide with fear.

The door did not move again. The animal outside was now silent. The creature had given up on its pursuit of him, or it was sat outside of the door and waiting patiently for its meal to re-appear. Either way, Alan was not going to be opening that door again for a while yet. He was stuck inside of the building until he found the company of other human beings, or until the relative safety of daylight came.

Alan allowed himself some time to get his breath back, and then he stood up using the wooden obstruction behind him for support. The counter that he had smacked his head on had been the reception desk. On the first appearance, this looked as if it was a guest house of some kind. On the desk, there was a visitor's book, and it was already opened, and the pages inside of the book were all empty.

He then noticed a brass bell perched on the edge of the desk. He rang the bell twice, and he waited patiently for an employee to come and attend to him. After waiting for what felt like an eternity, he rang the bell once more. This time he struck the bell repeatedly and much harder. He waited, but again there was still no response. It appeared as if he was in here on his own and that there was no one else at home.

The first thing that he decided to do was to

look around for a telephone that he could use to call for help. If this were a guest house, then surely they would have a phone inside? Alan walked around to the back of the counter. He looked all over the sides and underneath the desk. There was no phone anywhere that he could see.

To the left of where he now stood, there was a wooden door that was closed. He assumed that this must have been the door to the main office, but there were no signs on it. His fist rapped on the door noisily, and then he waited for a few seconds. There was no response from inside. He decided that he should try the handle to see if it was open.

He turned the circular brass handle around slowly, and he found that the door was unlocked. He pushed it open gently, half expecting to see someone asleep on the inside of the room, but as he opened up the door fully, he could see that the room was empty. On the wall, there was a cabinet of empty letter slots and a key cabinet with five keys hanging up on individual brass hooks. On the top of the solitary desk in the office, there was an old-style rotary dial telephone. He breathed a huge sigh of relief when he found it.

He picked up the telephone receiver and listened for a dialling tone. There was nothing though, not even the sound of static in his ear. The line was completely dead. He pressed the levers on the top of the phone up and down a few times, but the line was still silent. He replaced the handset on its cradle and just shrugged his shoulders. He was going to be stuck here alone for the whole night, or so it would seem.

Is anybody hungry?

Alan walked back out into the reception area. The building was fairly quiet inside, not like a lot of creaky old buildings that moved. There was a small open fire burning to his left. Occasionally there was the sound of fragments of loose soot dropping down from the chimney and into the fire. They then crackled away merrily in the heart of the flames. It had appeared as if there was no one at home, but he would have to explore all of the rooms in the guest house to check and to make sure. It seemed odd that the fire was still burning away without anyone being in here to tend it?

To his right, two doors were next to each other, and there was also a staircase and a bookshelf filled with rows of very old-looking books. Alan walked over to the bookcase, and then he noticed that none of the books appeared to have any titles printed on them, and that seemed more than just odd. He picked one of the books out from the shelf at random, and he opened up the leather-bound book. It looked and felt very expensive as he cradled it within his hands.

Inside of the book, the pages had yellowed with age, as if the book had been exposed to sunlight over many years. Oddly though, there appeared to be nothing printed on any of the pages at all. He flicked through the rest of the book, opening some of the other pages at random, but the pages were all the same. They were all blank.

He closed the book and replaced it into space and then he picked up another one from another shelf. There was nothing printed on the inside of this one either.

"What the fuck is going on here?" He said out loud. It was almost as if this was an elaborate stage set up that he now found himself in which was full of vanilla props. Why would someone keep a bookshelf full of empty books he wondered?

After returning the second book into its former position, Alan then walked over towards the double set of doors. There was nothing marked on either of them. He knocked on the first door three times. The knock was loud enough to alert anyone who might have been on the other side. He waited for a few seconds, but there was no reply.

The brass handle on the door was tarnished. It showed visible signs of age, but it was still clean. Alan reached out for the handle and gently pushed it down to see if it was accessible. The door was unlocked just as the office door was, and he slowly and cautiously opened the door. The room that he entered into was very dark. There was an old lamp fixed up on the wall, but the candle inside of it was unlit. Apart from that, he couldn't see a damn thing

It was obvious that he was going to need some light for him to continue his search around the building, so Alan made his way back over to one of the lit lanterns that was attached to the reception wall and he carefully lifted it down from its stand. He held the lamp out in front of his face, and then he walked back over towards the door.

The lamp was a lot heavier than he thought it would be, but he held it aloft in front of his face as he walked slowly into the room. He walked forwards for a few feet, and he found where the wall ended. The only way forward was for him to turn to the right. In front of him, he saw three urinals that were attached to the wall. It was only now that he started to smell the strong scent of ammonia, and it came at him in a sudden and overpowering wave that caused him to feel nauseous.

He then jumped a little as he heard the sudden sound of water splashing from over to his right-hand side, as the noise startled him. He swung the lamp around to see if he could spot from where the sounds were coming. There was a toilet cubicle right in front of him, but the door was closed. The door was not locked. The splashing sound was coming from the other side of that door.

Alan gathered his breath.

"Is there anyone in there?" He asked. Then the splashing sounds behind the door ceased instantly. He pushed the door gently with his finger, and it creaked as it opened. He pushed the door until it was fully open, but there was no one inside the toilet.

He moved further forward into the cubicle so that he could take a closer look down into the bowl. His curiosity was getting the better of him. As he leant forward, he could see that something was glistening in the water. It was shiny and dark, and it was moving. He lowered the lantern down to afford him a better view, and then the animal that was in the toilet, launched itself out of the water, aiming directly at his throat. It was an enormous rat that was now trying to attack him!

This was like no rat he had ever seen before. It

was big enough to be a very large cat or a medium-sized dog. The cornered animal had launched itself out from the inside of the toilet bowl with blinding speed. God only knew what it was doing in there in the first place. Alan didn't even want to think about it. He had no time to think about it anyway.

He instinctively batted the animal away with his fist as it jumped through the air straight towards him. The animal's teeth were razor-sharp, and they scratched the back of his hand as it was deflected away, and it struck against the toilet wall. The animal fell onto the floor, dazed from the blow to its head. It would not be dazed for very long though. Alan was already heading back towards the door, and as he ran out into the hallway, he heard the sound of the animal's feet as it scuttled across the smoothly tiled floor behind him.

He was now convinced that there was something wrong with all of the animals within this village. Both of the animals that he had encountered so far, were much larger than normal, and both of them had been aggressive towards him. He wanted to get out of this house, but he was certain that it still wasn't safe to go back outside. Given the option of standing up to either of the animals, he would rather face the rat again, but not if he didn't have to. Alan slammed the toilet door shut before the animal could come out after him.

Alan now faced another dilemma. He wanted to explore the other rooms of the house to find other occupants, but he had to be wary of hidden dangers that might be lurking behind any one of the other doors. He knew that he was just going to have to be brave and get on with it, but it would be better if he had something he could defend himself with though. He took another quick look around the reception, area and on back of the desk, he saw a silver letter opener propped up in its stand.

It wasn't exactly what he was looking for, but it would suffice as a makeshift weapon. He picked up the opener, and he felt that the surface was not smooth. There was something inscribed on the opener. It was engraved with the words 'The Halfway House.' He assumed that it must be the name of the guest house that he now found himself trapped inside.

Brandishing the weapon out in front of him, he walked toward the door next to the one that he had just exited. He was still carrying the lamp in his other hand. Awkwardly he managed to the handle down with the hand that same hand. He opened up the door just a little, and he raised the lamp up and out in front of him. The scent of the room was similar to the one next door. It was the ladies toilet. It made perfect sense that they would be placed next to each other.

Then he heard the sound of tiny feet scratching across the tiled floor as they came running towards him. More rats were waiting inside of this toilet too, so Alan didn't need to go any further inside. He quickly turned back, and he closed the door to keep the rats contained. He placed the letter opener safely in his pocket, knowing that he would probably need it again later.

As he had pulled the toilet door handle closed, he suddenly saw movement at the other end of the reception. A figure was passing into the room at the end of the hallway just past the reception desk. It looked as if it was a male, and he was dressed in a black suit. Alan thought that the man looked like a waiter or a butler. It was a relief that he wasn't alone here after all.

"Wait!" Alan shouted out after him. The figure did not acknowledge his call. Instead, he entered the room ahead of him and then he closed the door behind him. Alan then started running down the corridor in pursuit of the stranger.

Dinner for one

The door flew open as Alan barged into the room. He now found himself standing in a luxurious looking dining room. A long rectangular oak dining table had been set, and it was lit up with candles that stood proudly in expensive-looking silver triple candelabras. On the table, there were containers of food that had all been covered over with silver serving dish lids. A solitary glass of red wine had been poured out into a glass by the seat at the head of the table, and the rest of the open bottle had been left right next to it.

"Where are you?" Alan shouted out. He was confused as to why the man was no longer inside the dining room.

He had only been a second or two behind him, and there was no way that he could not still be in here somewhere. There was no response, though. The room was completely silent. There was a clock hung up on the wall, but the hands were not moving. It had stopped at ten past eight. It was the same time that he had struck the potholes earlier. It was something of an odd coincidence, to say the least.

Whatever meal had been prepared in the serving dishes, it smelt utterly delicious. Given what he had just endured, Alan had all but forgotten that he was hungry. It felt like someone was playing a game with him; he was pretty sure of it. 'Let them play.' He said to himself. He walked around to the head of the table, and then he slowly lifted the lid of the serving dish.

Underneath the lid, there was a large steak that was steaming, and it looked truly succulent. He picked up a steak knife and a fork, and then he cut into the meat. It was medium-rare inside. That was just the way that he liked it. It was surrounded on the plate by a generous amount of buttered new potatoes, a selection of fresh vegetables, and a gravy boat of piping hot gravy was sitting right in the middle of the table. They were his favourite foods.

Alan decided that he was going to play along with whatever game that this was. He walked around to the head of the table and lifted the glass of wine to his nose. He smelt it, and it seemed fine, so he took a small sip. It tasted like an Australian Merlot. That was his favourite choice of wine. It seemed as if whoever had arranged this meal for him, had taken some time to discover what his favourite things were. Impossible as it seemed, they knew what he liked to eat and drink.

If this was a game that someone was playing with him, then he was too hungry to care anymore.

"Fuck it." He said, pulling the chair out from under the table, and then he sat down. He picked a serviette up from the table and then tucked it into his shirt. He picked up the knife and fork again, and he worked his way through most of the meal. By the time he had eaten his fill, he had also polished off over half of the bottle of wine too. Afterwards, he belched loudly, and it left a horrid metallic taste in his mouth.

His stomach was full, and now he felt a little uncomfortable. He stood up from the table and made his way over towards an unexplored door at the far end of the room. He cautiously opened it up and then walked on through into what turned out to be the kitchen. There was no one in the here either.

The kitchen looked as if it hadn't been cleaned in a very long time. Cobwebs were hanging from the ceiling, and it was cold in there too. There were a few dishes in the sink, and they looked as if they had also been there for a long while. There was a large silver industrial appliance in the corner that Alan recognised. He walked on over to the fridge, and he opened up the door.

He was not prepared for the shock of what he

was about to find inside. The inside light was off, and there was no electrical power to the appliance. The food inside was not just rotten. It was decomposing and thoroughly riddled with maggots. The meat inside of the fridge was covered in a thick green mould, and the stench coming from the rotten food inside of it struck him like an iron bar to the face. It was horrendous.

He rushed over to the sink. Alan could not hold back the bile that was now rising from his stomach, and it touched the inside of his throat. The taste of the warm acidic fluid in his throat was a sensation that he knew very well. He was powerless to stop the projectile vomit that flowed out from his open mouth. The acid burned his throat as lumps of partially digested food fell into the sink. He ran both of the taps to try and wash some of the sick away down the plughole.

He vomited several more times before he eventually began to dry retch. His stomach felt as if it was almost empty, but now he was in a lot of pain. This was another sensation that he had experienced before. His stomach began to make odd gurgling sounds that could only mean one thing. He had to find a toilet, and he had to find one very quickly.

Room

The door that led back into the dining room burst open as Alan ran through it as fast as his feet could carry him. He was stopped dead in his tracks by the sight that was now on the table before him. The last of the food that he had left on the table was now also decomposing. There were maggots and flies crawling all over the rotting remnants that he had just left on his plate. It was a sight that sickened him. He thought about the flies vomiting all over the food that he had just eaten. Dead insects were floating in the bottle of wine as well.

He may have thought that his stomach was empty, but he quickly found out that it wasn't. He vomited on the spot, and as the bilious fluid flowed out from his mouth, it splashed right across the table. The smell of his vomit seemed to be getting stronger every time that he breathed inward. He was sick again, and this time it sprayed all over the dining room floor. There was so much vomit coming out of his body that he feared that it might not ever stop.

Then the unthinkable happened. The stomach cramps became so unbearable that his bowel opened up and he soiled his boxer shorts. He was unable to hold it in, and he felt disgusted with himself. Now he would need to clean himself up. If he encountered anyone else in the guest house, he doubted that he would be able to hide his embarrassment.

He shuffled through to the reception, trying not to let any more of the excrement flow out from his body. It was awkward trying to clench his cheeks together whilst his pants were partially filled with waste. He felt like a child who had just soiled his nappy and his face was bright red. Behind the reception in the office, he knew that there was a selection of room keys hung up on the hooks. Each of them was numbered from one through to five.

Alan picked up the key marked number one. He took a quick over at the toilet doors he had walked into earlier. They were both no go areas. He didn't fancy facing the angry rats again, no matter how desperate he was. He started to ascend the stairs carefully, and he eventually managed to climb up to the top.

He now found himself standing in a long hallway that again dimly lit with that same weak candle powered lamps. He wondered to himself, what had happened to the electricity in the village? It seemed to have very old fashioned decor here in the house. It looked very gothic upstairs, and the burgundy patterned wallpaper along the hallway looked to be very aged.

Alan carefully shuffled his way along the landing until he reached the bedroom door marked up with a brass number 'one' screwed into it. All five of the bedrooms were situated only along just one side of the hallway, and it seemed an odd layout. He placed the key in the lock and turned it around. The latch clicked as it became unlocked, and he entered the room hastily. He was no longer worried about what may be waiting on the other side of the doors for him. He just wanted to get himself cleaned up above everything else.

The room had quite a simple layout. It had a bed, a dressing table and two bedside cabinets inside of it. There was no television or telephone in there. Oddly enough, there didn't appear to be any plug points anywhere within the room either. This was one of the strangest guest houses that he had ever encountered. It was so dated that it felt as if it belonged in another century.

On the far side of the room, there was an open door. Alan could see that there was an older style bathtub inside. He needed a shower badly, but there wasn't even a shower mixer tap. At least he could now clean himself up though, and that was a blessing. He locked the bedroom door behind him and then he walked into the bathroom.

He closed the bathroom door behind him and turned on both of the taps to run the bath. Then he carefully started to take off his clothes. He grimaced as he sat down on the toilet and he just had to let go. It now felt as if his entire stomach was falling out into the water below.

He took his time, and he felt a huge relief when his stomach was finally empty. He cleaned himself up, and then he washed out his clothes using an old bar of soap that had been left on the sink. It wasn't ideal, but he had no other clothes with him. He would just have to make do.

He was almost sick again as he washed his boxer shorts clean. He was still disgusted with himself. Once he was happy that his clothes were as clean as he was going to get them, he hung them up to dry over the bathroom door and then he turned around and stepped on into the hot bath.

The water was just about at the perfect

temperature. It would have been a little nicer if he had some bubble bath to add to the water, but all there was to hand was another partly used bar of soap perched on the side of the bath. He sank slowly into the water, and finally, he felt able to relax. He lay motionless in the water for a while and just stared up at the ceiling. The flames from the candles were casting hypnotic shadows over the top of his head, and he watched the dancing images as they moved around above him.

He let the warmth of the water soothe his aching and tired body. He then soaped himself down, and it made him feel so much better. The warm water was helping the last of his stomach cramps to subside as well. Now he was sure that his mind must have been playing tricks on him. The food had looked and smelt incredible when he had eaten it. He now thought that he might be hallucinating due to food poisoning, or perhaps he just had a nasty bug of some kind? He closed his eyes for just a few seconds to relax for a little longer.

He had been in the bath for over half an hour. He stayed there until the water became lukewarm, and then he had decided that it was time for him to get out. As he stepped out of the bath, he was grateful that there was a towel folded up on the shelf above the bath. He picked it up and held it to his face. It smelt a little odd. It was not that it was dirty; it just smelt aged. That was probably the best way to describe it. He towelled himself dry, starting at his head and then working his way down the rest of his body.

When he was content that he was as dry as he was going to get, he wrapped the damp towel around his waist. He lifted his boxer shorts down from above the door, but to his annoyance, they were still soaking wet. He was grateful that he had the towel to keep around him. He picked up another small towel from high up on the shelf, and he used it to dry his hair. It was going to be a long night if he was stuck here in this room without anything to entertain him. If only there were a television, then he could at least find something to watch. If he had more power in his phone, he could have listened to some of his music, but there was no power, so that was impossible too.

As Alan had walked out of the bathroom, he was still drying his hair. The room now seemed much brighter than it had before, and as he removed the towel from his face, he dropped it down to the floor in shock at what he was seeing. He was apparently no longer still in the guest house anymore. He recognised where he was now, though. He was back in the bedroom of the house that he lived in when he was just sixteen years old.

"What the fuck is going on here! Who is messing with me?" He shouted out loud.

He assumed that this was possibly one of the most elaborate pranks ever played, or that he must be dreaming. He looked all around the room, and it was just how he remembered it. It was painted in the same colours, and there were those Duran Duran posters stuck up on the walls for decoration. Those same posters were the ones that his friends had once ridiculed him for displaying proudly. Why the hell did he have pictures of a male band on his wall they would often ask him teasingly?

Now and again, someone would refer to his sexuality and suggest that he was gay. It was never said in any seriousness, but it was enough to drive him mad. He wasn't gay, but he had friends who were, and he had no issue with who people chose to fall in love with at all. He simply idolised the band, and he loved their music. The lyrics spoke volumes to him. The band helped him survive his awkward teenage years, and the music would stay with him throughout all of his life. He was angry that he had to justify his choice of music over and over again. It had carried on like that for years.

He felt a sudden wave of nostalgia washing over him. If this was a dream that was taking him back to the years of his youth, then it felt incredibly real. There was a small portable television on the side, which was next to a large stack of hi-fi separates. His music set up was his pride and joy, and it had made him the envy of all of his friends.

On the far side of the room was his weight bench, and there was a punchbag hanging down from the ceiling, and smack in the middle of the room, there was his first-ever double bed. It was that bed, where he had first lost his virginity in a clumsy, fumbled attempt that had been all over in a record-breaking embarrassingly short space of time.

He had hardly been a favourite with the girls. He had drifted into numerous long term relationships back then. He had often found it hard to let go. He felt comfortable when he was in relationships, but he became desperately lonely when they had ended, and he found himself on his own again. It wasn't until he was in his late forties that he finally felt comfortable living on his own, but he had to survive a bitter break up before he could truly learn how to enjoy his own company.

Suddenly there was a loud knocking sound on his bedroom door, and it made him jump.

"Alan, it's me." The voice on the other side of the door said. He thought that he recognised the sound of the woman's voice, but it couldn't be her. It was impossible. She had passed away a long time ago, and how he had mourned her passing too. Now he was sure that this was all just an insanely perverse dream.

He just had to see where this crazy dream led him to, so he opened up the door, and there she was. She looked just as he remembered her and she was smiling at him. His ex-girlfriend Tanya who had passed away years earlier, was now standing right in front of him, in the hallway of his parent’s old house.

Tanya had a unique style at was all her own; she refused to be a slave to fashionable trends; she much preferred to do her own thing. She always wore a green neck scarf, even when it was warm. She loved her baggy jumpers too, and she would always wear very short skirts. Underneath the skirts, she would wear the nicest underwear, and occasionally she would wear fishnet stockings held up by a suspender belt. They turned him on massively, and he had always had a thing for them ever since.

She leant forwards and pecked him gently on the lips, and then she walked on into the room. Her touch felt real on his skin. He could now smell the sweet fragrance of her perfume as well. He had forgotten how much he loved the way that she smelt. She dropped her bag down by the door, and then she took off her neck scarf and placed it down on the bed. Alan was stunned on seeing her face again. She was truly beautiful to him. That relationship was the first time in his life that he had ever thought that he might be falling in love, and it felt incredible.

Tanya sat herself down on the bed, and then she smiled at him.

"Cheer up!" She said, and then she smiled even wider as she stared up at him. He knew just what that smile meant. It was more of a cheeky grin that told him that she was feeling horny, and she was both ready and eager to have sex. She suddenly jumped up from the bed and then made for her bag.

"I almost forgot. I bought you a present!" She said excitedly.

He already knew what the present that was in the bag was. He was reliving the same evening where he had made that monumental mistake that he had regretted ever since. He still remembered it clearly from all of those years ago. It was a memory that he had buried deep in the back of his mind. It had caused him a great deal of pain back then, so he had kept it buried. Tanya pulled the small black box out of her bag. She then handed it over to him; she gave him another huge smile as she did.

As Alan carefully opened up the jewellery box,

and there was a silver ring inside of it. It was engraved with the letters 'MAGS'. It was Tanya's nickname for him. He took the ring out of the box, and he placed it on the same finger that he used to wear it on. It fitted him almost perfectly. Its highly polished face reflected the light shining brightly on his bedroom ceiling.

"I love it." He said. It was the exact words that he had said to her back then. Then he leant forward and kissed her passionately, she opened up her mouth to meet his, and her tongue gently brushed against his tongue.

Tanya removed the towel that was wrapped around his waist and then she started to touch his penis. Her hand felt soft as it moved over his skin. She had always known how to excite him, and he had loved her. He just didn't know how much he had been in love with her, not until she was gone.

"Hold on a minute." She said. Then she slowly and seductively took her clothes off in front of him while he watched her undress.

She had started to put on quite a bit of weight recently. He couldn't help but notice it all over again as she had removed her top. She was happy with him, and she now felt comfortable being herself around him. She was eating out with him all the time, and he was partly responsible for her weight gain in the first place. Not that he would ever accept it, as he had started putting on some weight as well.

To see her naked body standing in front of him again, well it was like a dream come true. She now moved slowly towards him. She was wearing just her fishnet stocking and suspender belt. She took his hand, and then she guided it toward her vagina. Alan slipped two fingers gently into her, and he stroked his fingers inside her. Her moans of pleasure were growing louder by the second, and when she was almost at the point of climax, she pushed his hand away. She wasn't ready for that just yet.

Tanya then sat down on the edge of the bed, and Alan knelt on the floor so that he was in front of her. He started to kiss her on the knee of her left leg and then he began to move upward. Her body started to shiver in anticipation of his tongue finding its final goal. He worked his way upward slowly and teasingly until he was kissing her vagina, and then he started slipping his tongue all around and then in and out of her.

Tanya was moaning heavily. So heavily that he worried his parents might be able to hear her from the living room downstairs. Alan then placed one of his fingers in her mouth; it was one of the two that had just been inside of her. She sucked his finger hard, and she refused to let it out of her mouth. She loved her taste. She turned him on more than any other woman he had been with throughout his life. He missed her touch, her taste and her scent. He had forgotten just how special she was to him.

She then rolled over and carefully moved off the edge of the bed. Then she walked right in front of him as he stood upright in front of her and she turned him around and then pushed him back so that he fell on the bed. She straddled across him and used her hand to guide him inside of her. He thrust upward so he could get deeper inside of her, and she met with his thrusts.

"You're getting heavy." He said. Those three stupid fucking words had come out of his mouth all over again. He could not stop himself from repeating that same mistake from his past.

He had no idea why he had just said those words to her for a second time. It had been around thirty years since he had first said them, and he had regretted them every day since. She started to cry silent tears that he had not even noticed at the time, and she continued to grind down on his erect penis. She pretended not to care about his words, but Alan now knew the damage that he had done to the poor girl back then.

Tanya began to move faster and faster as she built toward an almighty climax.

"I'm so sorry," Alan said. "I never meant to say that." He meant it too. It was too late, though. He had never said sorry to her back then if he had then she might still be alive. Tanya had suffered from an eating disorder from a very young age. Now that she was in love, she felt able to eat finally. His words had cut her to the bone, and the man that she had fallen in love with, had now broken her completely with just those three little thoughtless words that he had uttered.

She placed her hand over his mouth, and then she moved faster and faster on top of him. If only he could have taken those words back, he would have done anything to do so, but now he had just hurt her all over again. Then he noticed that her body was starting to become thinner while she was still on top of him.

Her stomach started to shrink, and her bones

then started to protrude outward from underneath of her skin. As she ground down on him, he could now see her rib cage. Her arms were becoming so thin, that he could see her veins were now sticking out of them. Her hand was still tightly clamped over his mouth, and she refused to let go. Her grip was incredibly strong. He tried to push her off, but her body felt incredibly heavy despite how skinny she was now becoming.

Tanya sucked in her cheekbones, and they never came back out again. Her eyes then became surrounded by dark circles, and she was still moaning loudly. The skin on her body then started to turn a grey colour, and her body was so emaciated that he could see her entire skeleton. Then her skin started to turn to dust.

Her skin was now burning, just as her young body had burnt all those years ago when her young body had been cremated in her coffin. She slipped her fingers into his mouth for him to suck on them, and he almost gagged as his throat filled up with ash. Then she collapsed to nothing, and a layer of her warm ashes fell right across him.

Alan screamed an inhuman scream, and he rolled over on the bed. His breathing was now frantic, and he could not catch his breath. He jumped up from the bed, and he searched all around the dimly lit room. He was now back in the bedroom of the guest house again. Tanya was no longer here. There was no way that she could have ever been here. She was long dead. It was a nightmare that had felt so real that he now had tears welling up in his eyes.

Tanya had ended the relationship after she had left his house that night. She had been too ashamed ever to return. She could not bear to let him see her naked body ever again. He had tried to apologise over and over again, but it was no good. If only he had realised then, how much those words had hurt her. She would no longer take his calls, and the handwritten letters that he sent to her all went unanswered. He never saw her again while she was still alive.

Feeling betrayed by the only man she had ever loved and utterly ashamed of her body, she had stopped eating completely. Within six weeks, she had been hospitalised. Then she had taken an overdose of pills one night, and she had never woken up again. She died weighing just under four stone. When he heard the news about her passing, Alan had walked down to the lakes by his house, and he had cried his eyes out. They had often walked these lakes hand in hand, and here they had discussed a possible future together. She had been deliriously happy back then, and he had spoilt it all.

He stood by the edge of the lake, and he had taken the silver ring that she had given him from his finger. After kissing it, he threw the ring out into the middle of the lake. As far as he knew, it was still out there somewhere. It was the last remnant of his lost love, and he no longer felt worthy of the gift of love that she had given to him. He would think of her every time that he walked those lakes. He never forgot her face. He never fully forgave himself either. He thought that he was over her, but he wasn't. He had just buried her memory deep in the back of his mind.

He couldn't stay in this room for a moment longer. He moved back quickly across the carpeted floor towards the bathroom, and he took the wet clothes down that he left hanging over the door. He hurriedly put them back on again. He no longer gave a damn about how wet they were. He had to get out of this room right now. When he was dressed, he made his way over to the door. He unlocked it using the key that was still in the lock. He then stepped out hurriedly into the hallway.

As he closed the door behind him, he did not see the green neck scarf that belonged to Tanya was still in the room. It had fallen off the edge of the bed, and it was now on the bedroom floor. As he had locked the door behind him, it started to fade to nothing.

Back out in the hallway, the candles now seemed to be burning away just a little bit brighter than before. He had locked the door to room number one behind him and then tried the handle just to ensure that the past that he had once buried was now safely locked away inside. He did it just to put his mind at rest. The ghostly reminder of that regrettable moment from his youth had unsettled him, and seeing Tanya fading away to nothing, had upset him a great deal. Whatever this place was, it seemed to know all about him. It knew his deepest darkest hidden secrets. It knew his entire past.

He slowly walked back down the stairs with his heavy heart full of regrets, and he walked back over to the reception desk. He thought about trying to take another look outside of the front door, but then he decided against it. The wolf might still be out there waiting for him, right outside of the door, just waiting for its moment to strike. He walked around to the back of the reception desk, and he placed the key to bedroom number one back up on the hook. His hand was shaking as he did so.

He was going to take all of the other four keys with him, but then he noticed another key that had been tucked away safely right at the end of the mail slots. It was hidden nicely away from prying eyes. He picked it up and examined it. It had the words 'Master Key' exquisitely labelled in handwritten calligraphy on the wooden fob.

He took the key into his hand, and then he walked back up the stairs again. There were no other rooms left for him to explore downstairs, so he thought that he might as well look in one of the other bedrooms. He wanted to try and find a decent room in which he could get some sleep for the night. It was still relatively early in the evening as far as he could gather, but after the emotional roller coaster that he had just ridden, he wanted to close his eyes and rest, even if it was just for a short while. He was soon back at the top of the stairs again, and he kept his head down, and he crept past room number one as quietly as he could.

As he made his way along the hallway, he passed the master key from one hand to the other. It felt cold as he held it in his fingers, and it looked as if it were well worn. It looked as if it had been used thousands of times before, but he thought that it was odd as there can't have been many visitors to this village. This place had very little to attract any outsiders here.

He reached the bedroom that was marked with the number two, and he placed the key inside of the lock. He suddenly had the strangest feeling that there might be someone else waiting for him just on the other side of the door, so he paused. He knocked on the door loudly and then waited for any sign of a response.

When there was no answer, he turned the key, and he heard the latch click to tell him that the lock was now undone. He took hold of the handle, and after drawing in a deep breath, he walked on into the room. He searched all around the room with his eyes. There was no sign of anyone else inside. He closed the door behind him, and then he locked it from the inside. Just to be safe, in case he fell asleep in there.

The second room was decorated in a slightly different manner to the first, but the layout and the furniture were almost identical inside, except for a broken wooden handle on the chest of drawers. He walked over to the drawers, and he opened them up one after the other. There was nothing inside of them, except for a single sheet of scented paper had been placed in each one. He hadn't seen anything like this since he had been young. It was something that his grandmother used to do. She would place the paper on the base of her drawers to scent the clothes that were kept inside of them.

The bed in the middle of the room looked welcoming, but he walked over to the bathroom just to make sure that that this room was empty. There was no one in there. There was nothing at all inside, except for the bath and sink, a few cobwebs on the ceiling, and a solitary spider that seemed to be feeding on the remnants of a dead fly that had been caught up in its web. The spider was slowly going about its business and enjoying its pre-prepared ready meal for one. Being wrapped up in a web while still alive and then slowly being digested, it wasn't a way that he would choose to go, not if he were given a choice.

Alan felt a little safer as he made his way back over to the bed. He sat down on the edge of it, and the bed squeaked beneath him under his weight. It wasn't the most comfortable thing that he had ever sat down on, but he was sure that it would suffice. All that was left to do was to wait here in this room until the morning, or until someone else appeared before he could try to leave this place.

He took off his shoes, and then he lay down flat

on the bed. The mattress seemed to mould itself around his body; he felt almost as if he was being held in a warm embrace. Slowly his eyes started to slip until he could no longer control the urge to sleep. Before he knew anything about it, he was snoring away noisily. All around him, the furniture and decor in the room silently started to move and to transform. They were now converting the room into something else. It would become another memory that he would not wish to see. The next thing that he knew, he was awoken to the sound of a woman crying noisily on the other side of the room.

He sat bolt upright in the bed, and he was now in unfamiliar surroundings that he took some time to recognise. The sound of the woman crying was unmistakable to him, though. It was the sound of his dead mother, and she was in tears. It was impossible, but those were her cries. Now his mother (who had been dead for the last three years), had begun to call out his name from across the other side of the room.

In the arms of the angels

The cries that his mother was making sounded as if they were almost inhuman. These were not just tears of pain that he was hearing from her. They were tears of desperation and immense sadness.

"Alan! Alan! Where are you, son?" His mother cried out loudly. Alan jumped up from the bed, and he ran over to her side.

"I'm here, mum!" He said, and he went to hold her hand within both of his. His hands passed straight through hers. She wasn't here, and this wasn't real. He was now in a solitary room in the nursing home in which he had placed his mother to live out the rest of her days.

A picture of his mother and father was stood in a tarnished silver frame placed right next to her bed. A separate picture of Alan as a young child had been unevenly cut out from another old photograph using a blunt pair of scissors. The jagged edges were proof of just how useless the scissors were. The picture was tucked into the corner on the front of the photograph. She was only allowed to keep one picture frame close to the bed as she kept knocking them over accidentally when she had her night terrors. She was having another one of them now. Alan looked at the picture and how she had kept it so close to her bed. She might have missed her husband, but she missed her son even more.

She still had her old photo albums on the shelf on the other side of the room. Some days she would sit in the armchair by herself, and she would look back through her pictures. Some days she would remember the names of the people in those pictures; some days she could not recall who they were at all. It was the same on the last day that Alan had visited her, and now the memories of that day all came flooding back to him.

It was only a half-hour drive away from his

house to the home where his mother resided. Despite the relatively short distance, he seldom visited her. He had little time now for the woman who had brought him into this world. This was the woman who had virtually brought him up single-handedly. She was the woman who taught him how to read and write. She was the first person who had ever shown him unrelenting love and devotion. Now he had to force himself just to go and visit her.

He kept on making excuses to himself as to why he couldn't go and see her. Either he was too busy at work, or he had problems with the car that he needed to sort out. Sometimes he would use a pretend illness just to get out of visiting her. The reality of the situation was that she simply drove him insane. She could hardly remember anything, and she complained relentlessly about wanting to leave the nursing home. He thought that she was so ungrateful, as this was one of the better homes in the area.

She wanted to come home and live with Alan,

but that just would not fit in with his lifestyle. He would have to re-arrange everything to tend to her needs. She had often wandered off by herself, and three times in the past he had had to call the police to try and find her when she had gone off on a little jaunt, and no one could locate her. It should have been a heartbreaking decision to have to place her in a home, but to Alan, it had come as a major relief. He wasn't ashamed of it either. It was for the best he had told himself.

He remembered the last time that he had ever seen her alive. He had made the drive down to the home on a Saturday, and he had parked his car up in the car park outside of the home. He had picked up the supermarket flowers from the floor in front of the passenger seat, and he peeled off the five-pound price tag from the wrapper. He was annoyed that the checkout assistant had not done this for him. She hadn't even asked him if she should.

He felt that it was his duty as her son to take

her some flowers when he visited, but he hated spending money on things that were going to fade away to nothing within just a few days. Five pounds was an acceptable amount, and it would make her happy. Even though it was only a token effort, she would appreciate them.

He climbed the steps at the front of the building, and he walked into the reception where he signed his name in the visitor's book that was opened up on the counter. He exchanged a little banter with one of the brunette nurses, and then he walked on through to the private room where his mother now lived alone. She was sitting motionless in the armchair over by the window. She did not even acknowledge his presence as he walked into the room. Her memory was getting worse by the day.

He pulled up a chair and then he sat down in front of her.

"I got you some flowers, mum." He said, and then he tried to hand the bunch over to her. She stared at him blankly, hardly recognising that she was being spoken to, and then she looked away. He wasn't sure if she honestly didn't know who he was, or if she didn’t care that he was here. Perhaps she was just angry at him again for leaving her in here alone?

He realised that she wasn't going to take the flowers from him, so he placed them down on the floor, tucking them safely underneath his chair. He would put them in the vase for her before he left. He looked to see what time it was on his watch. He couldn't believe that he was checking the time already. It was just gone midday. He planned to be out of there by half-past twelve at the very latest.

His mother looked up at him through tired and bloodshot eyes. She looked as if she had been crying a lot recently. She had large bags under her eyes too. They probably needed to give her some stronger medication to help her sleep better he thought to himself.

"Who are you?" She asked angrily. She didn't recognise him after all.

"It's me, mum. It's Alan." He said, and then he tried to take hold of her hand. She quickly pulled her hand back away from him.

Her hands and arms looked skinny and frail. The skin on her hands was covered with purple marks. They may have been bruises or liver spots. He had no way of telling. He hated seeing her like this. She never smiled anymore. She always seemed to be in pain, and she had no real quality of life. Sometimes he thought that she might be better off if she passed. At least then her pain would all be over.

Who was he kidding? What he meant was that it would be so much easier for him if she weren't around any more. She would no longer be such a financial burden on him. This home was costing him an absolute fortune. He had sold her home, and the small amount of money that was left from that sale was dwindling very rapidly.

He would soon be left with nothing. Then he would have to start paying for the care out of his own money. It was grating him a great deal. He firmly believed that he shouldn't have to pay for this at all. His mother had worked hard and paid her dues for all of her life. What other choice did he have? She was his mother, after all.

His train of thought changed as he smelt something heavy hanging in the air. It was growing stronger. She was now smiling at him as she carried on straining as she soiled herself. Now she was sitting in her excrement, and the thought of it was making him feel sick. He pushed the buzzer to alert the nurses that they were needed in the room urgently. He couldn't face dealing with this anymore.

He held his breath, and then he leaned forward and kissed her on the forehead.

"I love you, mum." He said. He meant it too. He somehow knew in the back of his mind that he would probably never see his mother alive again.

He dismissed the thought from his head as a ridiculous one, and yet he had been right about these things in the past.

As the brunette nurse that he had been flirting with came into the room, Alan told her that his mother needed to be cleaned up. She had just had a small accident. Only when he was about to leave the room did his mother finally recognised him.

"Alan." She said in a quiet voice. He turned his back on her. He was unable to face her or deal with this anymore. This episode was the last straw for him. "Please take me home son. I just want to go home." She pleaded. Alan stopped dead for a few seconds, and then he carried on walking forward until he was out of the room and then out of the front door of the home. He climbed into his car, and he drove ever without ever looking back.

He was now in that very same room that he swore he would never step foot in again. His mother was now staring up at the pictures of the three of them. She had tears in her eyes. The bedsheets stunk of urine. She had been left alone for hours. It had leaked out from her adult nappy, and now she was lying in her own urine. She was so infirm that she was unable to get up by herself. She leant over to reach for the buzzer with which to call her nurse for assistance.

"Don't do it, mum!" Alan tried to warn her. He knew what was coming next, and this room was forcing him to see it for himself. It was no good trying to warn her. She was already long dead, and this was a recollection of an event from the past that he could not change, no matter how much he wanted to.

He watched his mother falling out of the bed and heard how she cried out as she landed down on the floor. "Help me. Help me, please!" She begged, but no one was coming to her aid. She was now sobbing loudly. The nurse on reception was sat with her feet up on the side while she was listening to music on her headphones.

Everyone was safely in their beds, and unless the patients warning lights flashed up on the wall, she wasn't going to be moving from her chair for a long time yet.

It would be another hour before she would do her next round of checks, but by that time, it would already be too late for her to save his mother.

"Help her!" Alan shouted out as loudly as he could. No one could hear his cries. He wasn't there. That was something that he alone would have to come to terms with now. He wasn't there for her at the end when she had needed him the most. He imagined that the end of her life would have been very different. He should have been called to her bedside and allowed to say one last goodbye to her.

His mother then knocked into the table next to the bed. She was trying to nudge the buzzer off the side to call for help. The buzzer remained where it was, but her treasured picture fell next to her. The glass in the frame smashed and fell out onto the floor in jagged pieces. It was enough to break her resolve finally. She touched the picture of her son with tears flooding out of her eyes. Alan could only watch on helplessly. He already knew how this story was about to end, and it hurt him to know what was coming next.

She picked the picture up in her hand, and she kissed her son's image. His happy smiling face smiled back at her. He was such a good boy. He was such a loving child. She wished that he was here with her now.

"Take me home son. I just want to go home." She said again. Alan then dropped down to his knees beside her.

"I'm here, mum, I'm with you. Don't do this, mum. I'm coming for you; I'm coming to take you home!" He pleaded with her. He was talking to a long-dead ghost, who could not be reasoned with in any way.

His mother then picked up one of the jagged

pieces of broken glass, cutting her fingers as she gripped the broken fragment from the frame. Her face was now etched with pain.

"You can come and live with me; I will take care of you!" He tried to tell her. She could not hear his remorseful words, and the end of her life was inevitable. She drove the glass into her wrist, and she cried in pain as the sharp edge cut upward. Then she moved to the other wrist, and she did the same. Her face looked terrified as she realised what she had done, but there was no turning back for her now.

She must have had a last-minute change of heart. She looked as if she was panicking. She bashed her arm against the cupboard repeatedly. She was still trying to knock the buzzer down. On the third attempt it fell down to the floor, but it spun across the tiled floor, and it landed far out of her reach.

She was already weak. The blood was flowing steadily out from her veins, and the life was ebbing away from her body. The crimson fluid pooled around her body, and she was now bathed in her blood. Alan was sobbing his heart out as he watched on helplessly.

"I'm so sorry that I let you down mum. I love you so much!" He cried.

"I love you son." She said as she looked at the picture of her son for one last time. She smiled, and then she closed her eyes. She would never open them up again.

That was how she had been found an hour later. She was dead in a pool of her piss and blood. She was still holding the picture of her son tightly in her hand. She had died without dignity, and it broke Alan's heart to have to re-live it all over again. To have to see it first hand was even more agonising for him. He ran over towards the bedroom door. He was crying out in unfathomable pain.

He unlocked the door and ran out into the hallway, where he collapsed down onto the floor.

He was holding his head in his hands while he cried at his shameful actions. His mother had deserved to have been treated far better, and there was no one else to blame but himself.

Whatever this cursed place was, it knew him. It knew all of his demons. If this was all just a bad dream, then it was the most fucked up nightmare that he had ever experienced. It felt too real to be just a dream. This felt more like a reckoning for the mistakes that he had made in his life. He was now facing up to all of the regrets from his past. Visiting just two of the rooms out of the five had already left him a broken man. He wasn't sure if he even wanted to enter into any of the other bedrooms at all.

He was sat with his back to the wall for a while, and he let the last of his tears come out without any resistance. It was cathartic to cry. It helped him to face up to the mistakes from his past. He was genuinely sorry for what he had done. He sat motionless for a few moments, and then he placed his head in his hands, but he knew that he had to snap out of this.

He realised that there was no point in him just sitting there and wallowing in self-pity. It felt more and more as if he had been sent here to this guest house for a reason. The place knew his deepest secrets, but he thought that he knew this place had a secret too. He just couldn't work out why it felt so familiar to him. He was positive that he had never been anywhere like this before, not even as a child.

He stood up on his feet, and he wiped away the remnants of his tears away from his cheeks. His pain and remorse had been all too real. There were three more rooms left for him to explore. Nothing in those rooms could hurt him the way the pain of the last room had, and he was sure that he had nothing left to hide. He stood up and gathered his thoughts. He was now ready to face whatever lay behind bedroom door number three. He unlocked the door, and then he walked straight in.

Inside, room number three was a lot smaller than the first two rooms had been inside of previously. He hadn't knocked on the door, and there could have been someone inside for all he knew. He no longer cared about that now, but there was no one in here anyway. There was no en suite bathroom built onto the side of this room. In the middle of the room, there was just a single bed. There were children's toys placed all around the room. There were lots of dolls and other girl's toys. He was in a child's room, but there was no child in here.

He sat down on the bed in readiness for whatever it was that the room wanted to show him. He had nothing to feel guilty about concerning a young child. He was positive about that, so the fact that this was a young girl's room was now confusing him.

"Well...what are you waiting for?" He said out loud. The room remained silent. He looked all around, examining each of the walls. There was nothing to give him any clues in here. There were no pictures on the walls; there were just dolls scattered everywhere. It looked as if they were all watching him. They were placed all around the room. All of them sitting and facing the bed where he now sat.

He waited and waited. He was becoming more impatient by the second. Then he realised that he must be doing something different. He lay back on the bed, and he closed his eyes tightly. He waited for whatever it was that the room had to show him. He waited for a long time. He waited so long that he eventually fell asleep once again.

He was awakened by a small hand pulling at his hand. He opened his eyes, and he struggled to find his focus. This felt as if it were real. The child in the room felt as if she was yanking on his fingers. He had no idea who the young girl might have been though.

The girl must have been four or maybe five years old at the most. He sat up, and he looked at the girls face.

"Hello," Alan said. "Are your parents here in the

guest house?" He asked.

"Just my Daddy is here." The little girl replied. She was now smiling back at him. She looked so innocent, and Alan wondered if she were real or not. He wanted to try and find some answers as to what was going on. He doubted that the young girl would be able to help him out much, though.

"Do you live here?" He asked her. He was hoping that her parents might be somewhere close by to them. She laughed at the question that he was asking her.

"Nooooooo silly. I don't live here. I don't live anywhere!" She then walked over to the dolls and picked one up from the side. "This is Rebecca. She is my favourite!" She said excitedly.

None of this was making any sense whatsoever. Whatever this room was trying to show him, it was failing dramatically in its task.

"What's your name?" He asked her.

"My name is Atlanta!" She said as she hopped around the room in a circle with the doll firmly held in her right hand.

He knew of no children by that name. There was no one in his family with a child of that name either.

"How old are you Atlanta?" He asked. She took a little time to think. She placed her finger to her chin as if it would help her think more carefully.

"Erm, I think I should be five. If I were alive, that is." She answered. Then she dropped the doll down onto the floor.

Her head fell onto her chest, and she now walked slowly over to the window and stood with her back to him. The penny suddenly dropped, and Alan then realised the true purpose of the room. He shook his head in disbelief at what he now being shown. He now fully understood why he was here.

"Oh, dear God no." He said. He now knew that this room was going to hurt him as well.

Atlanta Rain.

It had happened almost six years ago. He had met a nice local girl who went by the name of Coral. It was an unusual name, but she was an unusual girl. She was what he called a free spirit. She was fairly ordinary looking, but there was something about her that had attracted her to him in a way that he hadn't been drawn to anyone else in a very long time.

The relationship had grown from strength to strength, and after just a few weeks of them being together, he had asked her to move into his house with him. His friends all loved her. She was something special, and everyone who met her would take an instant liking to her. To top all of that, the sex between them was incredible. She had such boundless energy that left him feeling exhausted every single time that they made love.

Over the next few months, Alan started

spending a lot of time more at work after receiving a promotion, and he became a little jealous of just how friendly she was with all of her friends, both the males and the females alike. She was very affectionate to everyone that she knew. She had told him all about her wild past and how she had experimented with people of the same sex when she was younger. She had always thought that it would excite him, but instead, it made him feel even more insecure about their relationship.

While he was working late, she would often stay out partying until the early hours of the morning, and her social circle was different from his. He soon realised that he was losing interest in her. That was compounded when met someone new, and they started meeting for nights out in secret. After he had slept with the new woman a few times while he was supposedly working late in the office, he decided that he was going to tell Coral that it was over. When he had told her that it was ending, then she had dropped that bombshell, in her inimitable way.

That day, she had walked straight in excitedly through the front door, and her face was a picture. She was beaming from ear to ear, and she had bright glowing skin. She was in a great mood, but Alan knew that he was going to spoil her evening. She rushed up to Alan and kissed him passionately with her open mouth, pressed firmly against his. He kissed her back, knowing full well that this would probably be the last time they that their lips would ever meet.

He wanted to fuck her just that one last time, but even he did not have it in him to lower himself that far. Then she had pulled something out of her pocket. He couldn't see what it was that she was holding in her hand, but knowing Coral, it could have been anything at all.

She then ran up the stairs carrying the mysterious item with her.

"I need to tell you something!" He shouted up the stairs after her.

"Just a minute, I need to go pee!" She shouted back down the stairs at him, and then he heard the bathroom door closing. She didn't lock it behind her; she never did. That was Coral.

In the bathroom, she pulled down her jeans and knickers and then she put the toilet seat down. She never complained about it being left up; it was easy enough to pull it back down again. Awkwardly she placed the item between her legs, and she let the urine flow over the end of it.

Some of her pee splashed up on to her fingers, but she wasn't worried. It would wash off easily enough. She then pulled the item out and using the hand without the pee on it, and she held it out in front of her face. The line slowly turned blue. She was pregnant. This was the third different test that she had taken today that had said she was, and she couldn't wait to share her exciting news with the father to be.

She had hoped that it would bring them much closer together, and perhaps he would finally realise that she was happy and ready to devote herself to him. She wanted them to become a permanent item, and for them to settle down with their new small family unit. Her biological clock was ticking away, and she had been thinking about wanting a child for a good while now. Alan knew that she wasn't using any protection, but he never seemed to care about that.

She washed her hands and then wrapped up the tester in a bundle of tissues. Then she opened up the door and walked out of the bathroom. The master bedroom door was open, and when she walked past, she looked into the room and saw what was on the bed. Her face suddenly dropped. Her suitcase was full, and carrier bags full of her clothes stood on the bed next to it.

She walked slowly down the stairs, and her face was filled with confusion. Alan was now standing with his back to her, and his head was lowered. He couldn't turn around to face her. She would know just by looking at his face that he had done something wrong. She just had a way of knowing these things.

"What the hell is going on?" She asked him. Her voice was low, but he could sense that she was angry.

He had never seen her angry before; he had never even heard her swear in anger before. Now he couldn't even turn around and tell her to her face.

"There's no easy way to say this Coral, so I am just going to come out with it. I've been seeing someone else, and we can't be together anymore. I'm sorry." He said. He was genuinely unhappy at having to tell her, and he was going to miss the incredible sex that they had shared, but people moved on. He was never in it for the long term anyway, and she should have known that.

"But we talked about having a baby?" She said, with tears already starting to well up in her eyes.

Her face was now becoming pale white. She wished that he would turn around so that he could see the pain that was now etched on her face.

"We talked about a lot of things. People change Coral, and this relationship has sadly run its course. I never thought that it would go as far as it did. I thought that we were just a short term thing. I'm sorry, but you have to leave. I guess you saw that I packed up all your things for you to save you the job. I thought it would be easier for you that way." He still could not turn around to face her. He was such a coward.

Coral placed the pregnancy test back in her pocket as she tried to fight back her tears. Her hands were shaking, and the realisation of what was happening was finally sinking in. It was over. There would be no future for them. There would be no family.

"Just answer me one question before I go. Have you fucked her?" She asked.

She hoped that there might still be a way that this could be resolved. Perhaps she could change his mind, and he might give the relationship a second chance. It couldn't be because of the child that she was carrying though. She couldn't tell him that she was pregnant; otherwise, she would feel that she had trapped him into staying with her.

She desperately wanted him to change his mind before it was too late, but she needed to hear the truth before she decided if she was walking away or not.

"Yes." He answered. There was no remorse in his answer. He was nonchalant, and he was still facing away from her. Part of her wanted to slap him around the face, but it was pointless. He just didn't want to be with her anymore.

"I will go and get my things." She said. She wasn't going to cry anymore. Not here, not now. He didn't deserve to see any of her tears. He wasn't the sort of man that she wanted as a role model for her child. He was a selfish pig who only thought about his own needs.

She carried her bags down the stairs, along with her suitcase that had been filled to bursting. She had left him a little present under her pillow. She hoped that when he found it, he might realise the damage that he had done. She doubted that he would care though. He would probably see it as a lucky escape. Before she left, he finally turned around to face her. She looked calm and collected. He didn't expect to see that. Then she smiled at him.

"If we did have a child together, I would have named him Simon if it had been a boy, after your favourite band's lead singer. If it were a girl, then we could have called her Atlanta after the bass player's daughter. Atlanta Rain. The name Rain would have been for me. She would have been just like me, you know, a free spirit. A light in a world filled with darkness." Coral said. She then unlocked the front door.

Alan was impressed with her choice of names, she had paid attention to all of his musical tastes, but she was talking about a future that would never be written. He was moving on, and Michelle was patiently waiting for him to call her and to tell her that he was ready for her to come over to his house for the first time. She didn't know anything about Coral. Telling her about his live-in girlfriend had slipped his mind.

"Goodbye, Alan. I hope this woman makes you happy. I doubt it though. You have a love for money and power, but nothing else." She said, and then she picked up her bags, and she took them out to her car.

He had no other words to say to her. There was not even a last goodbye. She was right about him. He was ambitious, and he was already climbing up that ladder of success. He was just glad that it was all over between them. She had been a distraction that he could no longer afford to entertain. It was going to be casual relationships and nothing else from now on.

Before Coral had even left the driveway, he had already called Michelle to tell her to come over. Within an hour, she was at his house and helping him to polish off two bottles of wine. She had ended up staying over for the night. When she woke up the next morning, her hands were underneath her pillow. Her head was pounding, and she needed a strong coffee. Then she touched something oddly shaped. She ran her fingers over it, and then she lifted the pillow up and took hold of it. Alan was fast asleep. He was snoring away with his back to her.

The kick in the small of his back was hard enough to wake him up. It was so forceful that it pushed him clean out of the king-size bed and down onto the floor where he landed with a thud. He stood upright in shock at what Michelle had just done to him.

"What the fuck was that all about?" He shouted at her, surprised at what had just happened, and at how sore his back now felt.

"What the fuck is this?" Michelle screamed at him, and she threw the pregnancy test in his face. It fell to the bedroom floor landing on the rug at his feet. It was the first time that he had seen it, and he had no idea what it was at all. He picked it up from the floor, and he examined it through his blurry hung-over eyes.

"Oh, fuck." He said. "But you can't be pregnant already. We've only fucked a few times!" He said, surprised.

"It only takes one time you fucking dickhead! One little sperm from those tiny testicles of yours is all it takes. The test isn't mine though you fucking idiotic prick!" She shouted at him furiously.

She reached out for anything that was close to hand, and she grabbed the first thing that she found. She threw her empty wine glass straight at him. It missed his head, but only narrowly. Michelle was now out of bed and getting dressed. There was nothing he could say to her that would calm her down. He had to speak to Coral, but until Michelle had left the house, it would be impossible.

Michelle had insisted that he drove her back to her home. That was a good twenty minutes drive away. Every mile that they drove was agonising for him. All he could think about was the way that he had treated Coral so callously the day before. The hurt and pain that had been etched on to her face that he had chosen to ignore, and now it had all made perfect sense. She had been deliriously happy, and he had broken her with his words and his selfish actions. He felt ashamed of himself.

When they finally arrived at Michelle's house, she got out of the car without saying a single word to him. She was furious at being used like that. She had slammed the car door behind her so hard, that the glass window juddered in the frame.

"Hey!" He protested at her, and she heard him

shouting at her from inside of the car. She angrily flipped her middle finger up at him, and then she started walking off towards her front door.

She had only walked a few steps towards the door when she seemed to change her mind, and she turned back around. Her face was now bright red, and she looked furious, she then ran back in the direction of the car, and Alan locked the doors as a precaution. She tried the car door handle and discovered that it was locked; it incensed her even further.

She kicked out at the door, leaving a large dent in it that would be costly to repair. Alan had now seen enough. He sped away from the drive, leaving her raging behind him. He could see her in the rearview mirror. He was stamping her feet and throwing things all over her garden. She was acting like a spoilt brat. He breathed a sigh of relief. This had been a lucky escape. That sort of woman was volatile and unpredictable. She was a heavy drinker too. He wasn't too keen on that.

It reminded him too much of some bad memories from his past.

He waited until he was a safe distance away, and then he parked up the car, and he tried calling Corals number. Her phone rang endlessly until it finally went through to her voicemail. He left her a message telling her how sorry he was and that they needed to talk, but she had never returned his call.

He did not hear from Coral for weeks after, and he eventually decided that it was time to move on with his life. If she turned up on the doorstep in a few months, along with his child, then he would do his best by her. He would pay her money if that were what she wanted. Eventually, he heard from one of her friends about what had happened to her. Coral had made the heartbreaking decision not to become a single mother, and she had terminated the pregnancy. She cried about the decision every single day for weeks on end.

Alan never saw Coral again. She was a free spirit, and she had quickly moved out of the area. He had no idea where she finally ended up. He just hoped that she was happy with her life. He thought about her from time to time, but any thoughts about the child that she was carrying had soon faded away. Now the spirit of his unborn daughter was standing in the room in front of him, and she looked just like a younger version of her mother, Coral.

He wanted to apologise to his daughter for what he had done or to pick her up in his arms to protect her, but she was the spirit of a dead child who had only briefly existed inside of her mother's womb. His choices had ended her existence before she had even taken her first breath, and he felt sick to his stomach. His child could have gone on to be anything in this world, she was special, but he had only thought about himself, and he never even gave her a chance to try.

Atlanta was now standing over by the bedroom

window, and she was keeping her back to him. It was just as he had done to Coral all those years ago. Atlanta then started talking to herself. She was reciting a poem that a child of her age should never even have known about at all. He recognised the words. It was called 'On a dead child' by Richard Middleton. Atlanta spoke every word beautifully and hauntingly, and Alan began to silently weep as he listened to the sorrow in her voice while she spoke.

"Man proposes, God in his time disposes,

And so I wandered up to where you lay,

A little rose among the little roses,

And no more dead than they.

It seemed your childish feet were tired of straying,

You did not greet me from your flower-strewn bed,

Yet still, I knew that you were only playing,

Playing at being dead.

I might have thought that you were really sleeping,

So quiet lay your eyelids to the sky,

So still your hair, but surely you were peeping,

And so I did not cry.

God knows, and in his proper time disposes,

And so I smiled and gently called your name,

Added my rose, to your sweet heap of roses,

And left you to your game."

Tears now rolled heavily down both of his cheeks. He had never felt so ashamed of himself in his entire life. He looked down at his hands as he held them out in front of him, and they were shaking badly with nerves.

"I'm so sorry for what I did to you Atlanta." He said. He was hoping that she may somehow find it in her heart to forgive him for what he had done. By the time that he had looked up again, she had already climbed out of the open bedroom window, and she was now standing out on the window ledge.

Time then seemed to move in slow motion. He jumped up from the bed shouting at the child as he ran towards her. "No, don’t do it!" He screamed at her. It was already too late. She had spread her arms out wide, and she had jumped out into the air, and she was now falling through the rain-filled sky.

As he reached the window ledge, he looked down frantically at the ground below. He searched from side to side, but there was no sign of a body to be seen. He couldn't see her anywhere, just like the line from the poem that she had recited. Then out of the window, he could now see fireflies that were now forming uniformly into the outline shape of his unborn daughter. They held the shape for a few seconds then they changed formation into that of a rose. They were dancing in the cool summer rain and illuminating the sky with the magical innocence of a child's imagination.

The fireflies flew off into the distance until he could no longer see them anymore. He hated himself for what he had done. He whispered a sorrow-filled goodbye into the cold night air.

"Goodbye, Atlanta Rain. Goodbye, my daughter." The words stuck in his throat. He closed the window down tightly. He then walked slowly back over to the door, and he let himself out of the room without looking back.

The candles dimmed in the room behind him all by themselves. One by one, all of the dolls then disappeared, and the room fell into total darkness. As he had closed the door behind him, in the darkness, a solitary firefly had appeared up at the window. It stayed outside for just the briefest of moments, and then it was gone.

After visiting the first three bedrooms, he had no idea what he was likely to expect in the fourth. He thought that he was finally starting to understand what this was all about though. The place held all of his deepest darkest memories and mistakes he had made, and they were showing him the errors of his ways.

There was very little that he could do about what had happened in the past, but when he left here, he would try to make up for his mistakes in some small ways. He had no idea how he was going to do that, but he would somehow find a way to ease the burden on any other people that he may have hurt over the years.

He let himself straight into the fourth bedroom, without even giving himself a chance to become composed for his next encounter. He no longer cared about what he would come to see in the room. He somehow knew that this would not be easy, but it would not be over for him until he had visited all five of the rooms. He closed the door behind him, but he did not lock it. There was no point in doing so anymore.

He already knew how to activate the purpose of the room, so he lay down on the bed and then he closed his eyes tightly shut. He waited there patiently for the next story to unfold, and it did not take long for it all to begin.

On the far side of the room, he heard the sound of the metallic cap on a bottle being twisted open. Then he heard the chink of glass on glass and then the sound of a liquid being poured into the glass. It was at that very moment that he knew who he was going to see when he opened up his eyes.

"Hello, Dad." He said. Then he opened his eyes as he sat upright, and he stared across the room at his late father. There was no reply to his greeting.

His father had already drunk his way through

three-quarters of the bottle of spirits. He replaced the cap on the bottle tightly. He did not want to knock the bottle over and lose the remainder of the drink during a drunken stumble. He had done that too many times before. The glass in front of him was now full again. He lifted it to his lips, and he took a small sip of the drink.

The room was virtually bare. There was no furniture in here. He had no television and no radio. There was nothing. There was just the man that he had once admired, along with a table and a chair and the clothes that his father had on his back. It was a poor way for anyone to exist. It looked like this was a homeless hostel somewhere in a deprived area.

Alan's father had left the family home when Alan was just nine years old. The reason for his leaving was clear. It was his love of alcohol. At first, he had been a social drinker. He had started down that path by drinking just the occasional glass of wine with his work colleagues. That had soon increased to him drinking a few bottles of wine each night.

Soon after that, he discovered that the wine was no longer having the desired effect, so he had moved on to stronger and harder drinks. Before he knew it, he was knocking back bottles of the harder spirits.

He had tried every spirit under the sun until he grew tired of them. Eventually, he had settled on whiskey as his favourite tipple. Alan hated the smell of it on his father's breath. He hated the man that his father was becoming in front of his eyes. His mother had hated it too.

When he was a child, he and his father had done a lot of fun things together. Alan had doted on his father back then. He was strong and active. He was naturally great at most sports that he put his hand to trying. Alan wanted to grow up to be just like his father. He was his hero.

On top of his athletic ability, he was also a very intelligent man, and he could hold his own in any conversation, and on top of that and more importantly to Alan, back then he was also a lot of fun to be around. He worked hard and found himself moving up in his company, and that was when the trouble for the family had started.

The higher up the ladder his father climbed, the more money he earned. The pressure of his workload increased, and with the increased demands came a need to work longer hours. That led to a great deal of pressure and stress on his shoulders. Alcohol was the tool that provided a release for him. It took the edge off of the pressure. He found that it helped him to relax.

He started to drift away from the family. Sometimes he would not even come back home at night at all. Alan's mother tried to protect her son as much as she could, but within just two years, it was clear that the marriage was in serious difficulties. It broke Alan's heart when he thought about not having both his mother and father around. The first time that his father had been asked to leave, Alan had cried himself to sleep every night for a week.

As is often the case when families are dealing with addiction, his father repeatedly promised his mother, that things would change. His mother agreed to try and resolve the issues, and she finally agreed to let him move back into the family home. For a while, it looked as if his father would stick to his word. He gave up the drink for a few weeks, and it appeared as if it was all going to be alright. They even got around to booking a family holiday for the three of them. They agreed that time away together would help them to bond and to heal properly. Alan felt that he had his father back at last.

A true sign of alcoholism is someone hiding the evidence of secret alcohol abuse. It wasn't long before his mother had started finding empty bottles hidden in the cupboards, under the sink, in the bathroom, and even in the airing cupboard in the hallway.

She had confronted her husband about it, and

he had denied it repeatedly. She wasn't stupid though; she could smell alcohol on his breath, and as it came out through the pores in his skin. She loved him, though, and it was difficult for her to let him go. She didn't want Alan to suffer again. She turned a blind eye and hoped that her husband would realise the error of his ways. He knew, but he just couldn't stop himself.

On one Friday night when things turned sour again, it was already gone eleven, and his father still wasn't home from work. Alan had sat up with his mother until just after ten, and then she had sent him up to bed. He had pretended to be asleep, but he was waiting for his father to come home. When his father finally stumbled in through the front door, Alan had wished that he had gone to sleep.

His father fell through the front door, and he had then collapsed in the hallway. His trousers were stained with his urine, and he had vomited all over his jacket. His mother had gone to help him up, but she could not lift him from the floor.

His speech was so slurred that he was mumbling incoherently about being sorry and saying something else that she couldn't understand. She had seen him drunk too many times, but he was in a much worse state than she had ever seen him before.

His mother had tried in vain to move him or to encourage him to get up from the floor. He wouldn’t move from where he had fallen. He was so out of it that she eventually decided to leave him where he was. She would clean him up in the morning. She took a blanket out from the airing cupboard for him, and she noticed yet another empty bottle hidden in there as she did so. She knew deep down that she could not take much more of this. It wasn't fair on any of them. She still loved him though, despite what he was putting them all through.

She covered him up with the blanket, and then she rolled him over and on to his side. He was still mumbling away, incoherently to himself. She kissed his forehead, and then she went up to bed alone. Alan had been watching it all from where he had been hiding up on the landing. His mother had hardly slept a wink that night.

Now and again, she would have to get out of bed just to check that her husband was alright. Twice he was sick during the night, and he would have no memory of it in the morning or any recollection of his wife cleaning the mess up from the carpet while he snored away next to her. She caught sight of herself in the hallway mirror. She looked aged beyond her years. This was all taking its toll on her health.

Alan came downstairs for breakfast at just gone eight. His father was already sat down at the family table. He was still in the same clothes that he had slept in, and Alan could smell the foul smells that were coming from his suit trousers and jacket. On the table, there was a glass of clear liquid filled right up to the top. Alan looked at the glass, and then at his father. He had a worried look on his face. His father must have seen his expression.

"Don't worry son. It's only water." He was lying to his son, and Alan knew it. The whiskey had all gone. The only alcohol that was left in the house was a bottle of vodka that had been given to his wife, the previous Christmas. She had only drunk one glass from the bottle during the entire year, and that was on her birthday.

Then there was a knock on the front door. Alan's mother was still in her dressing gown, and she was already on her way down the stairs. She answered the door, and she became worried about what was going on when she saw that it was two policemen who were stood on the doorstep. They asked her if her husband was at home, and she had said that he was. Then she had let them both in.

They had arrested her husband in the middle of the kitchen in front of both her and her son. Alan was crying and begging them not to take his father away. They placed his father in handcuffs, and then they had dragged him out of the house in shame. The nosy neighbours were already peering out of open doors and from behind twitching curtains.

The blue flashing lights on the police car had already attracted a lot of attention, as this was quite a well to do area. It wasn't very often they got to see anyone arrested and dragged out of their homes that early on a Saturday morning, and the rumour mill soon went into overdrive.

His father was released on bail later that day, but he had been charged with theft. He was given a date to appear in court, and he would have to return to the station regularly until the court date. He had been taking petty cash from the offices at his work to enable him to fund his drinking habit. They had been suspicious as money had been going astray for a while. At first, it was just paltry amounts; but recently, whoever was taking the money had become a lot greedier.

They had consulted a security firm, and on their advice, the company had installed a hidden camera, and his father had been caught in the act. He had been dragged into the manager's office, and there he was presented with the evidence. He begged for forgiveness and promised to pay back every penny, but they still dismissed him on the spot. They had also called the police to have him arrested, but the police had been so busy that they had not been able to attend that afternoon.

The company were glad to see the back of him. He was a major embarrassment in front of the clients. He always stank of drink, and despite the company trying their best to offer him help, he had become much worse over the last few months. The thefts from the cash tin were the last straw. He was barred from ever entering the building again.

When Alan's mother had found out why he had been arrested, she started going through all of the families financial statements. Her husband had always provided for them, and he paid all the bills on time, as far as she knew. He earned good money. She was horrified by what she had found out that day. Her husband had run up debts of over fifteen thousand pounds.

He had maxed out both of the family credit cards. On top of that, he had also taken out a huge overdraft, emptied the joint bank account, and he had even withdrawn the money from Alan's savings account. It was money that was meant to be set aside for their son’s future.

Then she was upset to see that the family holiday had also been cancelled and on the bank statement, there was an entry showing that the money had been refunded to their account. She would have to tell Alan that they weren't going to be able to go away on holiday now. It was the final straw. She decided that she was going to have to speak to a solicitor. Difficult as it might be for Alan to deal with, she wanted a divorce.

When his father had been released from the police station, he went straight to a local off-license and stole a bottle of whiskey from one of the shelves. He just couldn't help himself anymore. He needed the drink. He had then gone and sat in the park and drank the entire bottle in less than an hour. When he returned home, his wife refused to let him come back into the house. He had wandered off, shouting obscenities at her as he had walked away.

It was half-past twelve when his father returned to the family home again. He then started banging noisily on the front door. The pounding was relentless, but no one was going to answer the door or to let him in. Realising that he was deliberately being ignored, he started shouting up at his wife's bedroom window.

"Laura! Laura!" He slurred. "I want to see my son!" He shouted. She had heard him banging on the door, but she decided not to answer it. She couldn't forgive him anymore. She hoped that by ignoring him that he might decide to wander off again and find somewhere else to sleep for the night.

Some of the bedroom lights came on in the other houses in the neighbourhood, and the curtains started twitching again. Those nosy parkers just couldn't get enough of a good story.

The gossip mill would be rife between the other housewives the next morning, Laura was sure of it.

"Lauraaaaaaa!" He shouted out at the top of his voice. When she didn't answer him, he then started banging noisily on the front door yet again. He wasn't going to give up that easily. Laura covered her head with the pillow and waited for him just to go away.

Alan had been woken up by the commotion, and he had made his way over to his bedroom window. He had opened up the curtains slightly so that he could see outside, and he could see that his father was stumbling and swaying from side to side all over the front garden. He hated seeing his father like this. He wanted him to go away. He wanted his sober father to come back home again.

His father had noticed his son's curtains were moving, and that seemed to spur him on even more. He turned around and started banging on the door even louder, and he shouted out his wife's name again.

"Why don't you fuck off your drunken bum, some of us are trying to get some sleep!" A male voice shouted out in the darkness. It was one of the neighbours by the name of Jerry Tate. Jerry was a local builder, and it was well known that he didn't put up with any nonsense from anyone. He conducted his negotiations with his fists.

"Fuck you!" His father slurred without realising who it was that was shouting at him.

"I want to see my son. He's my son!" His father had shouted back.

The words were slurred and lengthened, but they were loud enough to be heard by almost everyone in the street. He had just made one of the biggest mistakes of his life. One of the other neighbours had already called the police, and this was going to be a dramatic night for everyone involved.

Alan watched on in horror as Jerry Tate ran out from the front door of his house. He was wearing a pair of boxer shorts and nothing else. His fists were already clenched, and Alan knew what was coming. The first punch that Jerry threw was enough to send Alan's father reeling back across the pavement as it connected.

"Daddy!" Alan shouted. He had to try and help his Dad. He was drunk, and he was a fool, but he was still his Dad. He ran down the stairs in his pyjamas, and he headed out of the front door. His mother heard the door closing, and she jumped out of bed and ran down the stairs after her son.

Tate was punching Alan's father about the head and face over and over again. His face was already swelling up, and he looked a bloodied mess. Alan was only small, but he had jumped on Tate's back, and now he was screaming at him.

"Get off my Daddy!" He screamed. Tate swatted

him off of him using the back of his hand. Alan flew across the path, and he landed awkwardly, He was in pain, as he had twisted his ankle when he had landed on the ground.

His father watched on helplessly; he was too drunk even to stand up, let alone to defend his son. His mother had then run over to her son, and she had cradled him in her arms. She would not let Tate get anywhere near him. She had a ferocious look in her eyes that Alan had never seen before. She would protect her young son at any cost.

Tate was still carrying on with his relentless assault when the police car had arrived. Then the brawl became Tate fighting against the police as he assaulted both of the officers who had attended. By then end of the night, Tate would have taken on six police officers, and seriously hurt five of them. Alan could only look at his father, who was now lying motionless on the floor in a bloodied mess.

That was his father. That mess of a man was once his hero. The man was once his world now he meant nothing to him anymore. Every image that he had ever built up of his father had been destroyed that night. His father was physically and mentally weak. He could no longer protect his family. He cared more about drinking than his wife and son. Alan could not shake the thoughts away from the inside of his head.

Alan then wished that his father was dead. In his eyes, he already was. The thought had made him burst into tears. When they took his father away in an ambulance, he swore that he would never speak to him again. From that moment on, he was good to his word. He never spoke to his father again while he was still alive. Now he was in the same room as the man he had come to despise, and he was watching the final moments of his sad and lonely existence.

His father lifted the glass to his lips, and he sipped some more of the whiskey down. After all this time, it still burned as it rolled down his throat. He could no longer afford to rush his drinks. There was a pile of letters on the table all postmarked with 'Return to sender'. He had written a letter to his son every month. Every single letter that he had ever sent to his son had always been returned to him unopened.

He picked the pen up in his hand, and he began to write yet another letter. Alan stood up and walked over to where his father was now sitting. He thought that he could still smell the alcohol oozing out from his father's pores. It was heavy on his breath. He stood looking over his father's shoulder as he hand wrote the last ever letter that he would send to his son.

My dearest Alan,

This might be the last letter that I ever write to you. My liver disease is in its final stages, and I have refused any further treatment. After the last transplant failed, I decided that enough was enough. I write to you every month, and although you never read my letters, it brings me comfort to know that one day when I am gone, then you might find the letters and you will understand just how sorry I am for what I did to you both.

I am never stopped loving you or your mother. I just became too weak to deal with my life. I thought that I was stronger than alcohol. I was wrong. By the time I realised how addicted I had become, it was already too late for me to stop. I did try, but I didn't try quite hard enough.

Alcoholism is a cruel disease that makes you weak and demands your attention. I have no excuses for what I did to our family. I only have regrets that I never got to say sorry to you in person. It was my job to be your protector and provider, and I failed you. I cannot tell you how much of a failure I feel. I only ever wanted the best in life for you.

My doctor tells me that without further treatment, I will probably die within a few days. I refuse to go into hospital and make myself a burden on anyone else. My race is run. I messed this up, and without my family by my side, I can never beat this. I am just too weak.

I know that you probably hate me, and I think you are right not to want to have me in your life. I've messed up everything, and I can't undo the damage that I caused. All I can do is to tell you that I am sorry for letting you down and that I love you and mum.

Please take care of mum for me when I am gone. I think about you both every single day, and I want you to know how proud I am of you. If you ever have children of your own, don't tell them anything about me, I don't deserve to be remembered. I'd rather be forgotten for the failure that I am.

Love you always, my son.

Dad

For the first time since he was nine years old, he could see the humanity that still existed in his father. He could see the pain that was in his eyes. Even though he was still drinking, he was able to write and to think rationally. He sensed that the regret in his father's words was real. He also felt his father's loneliness. He had nothing left to live for anymore. The two people who he loved the most in his life had both abandoned him. Alan's heart started to sink. He never thought he would feel guilty about his father's passing.

For the first time in many years, he regretted all of those years of not speaking to his father. He remembered when he had first heard that his father had died. He had simply shrugged his shoulders, and he had just carried on with his life. The man was a ghost to him. His wish had finally come true. His father meant nothing to him. As far as he was concerned, he had already died that night when he was nine years old. That is what he had told everyone about his father ever since.

He felt ashamed of the way that he had rejected his father. Only now did he fully understand the battle that his father had faced with alcohol. It was an illness that he was suffering with then. It was a cruel addiction that had spiralled out of control. Ultimately it became his death sentence.

His father had to find the strength to face his death alone, and with the small amount of dignity that he still had, he had used his dying wish to ask to be erased from history to spare his son’s shame. His father was still a strong man, after all. Alan had been wrong about him for a very long time.

"I'm sorry, Dad." He said from behind his father’s shoulders.

His father’s skin was a yellow colour, and his jaundiced eyes were even worse. He was fading away fast, and the alcohol would numb his pain. He would be found alone in this chair, but not until months after his death.

The body of his father then started to decompose in front of him just as his body had done in real life. Maggots started to grow, and they began eating on his dead flesh. No one in the flats had wanted to touch the body when he was finally found. Alan watched his father's body fading away until there was nothing left that looked even remotely like the man that he once knew and idolised.

The room then started to change shape all around him again. This time he didn't even need to close his eyes for the room to start to warp. When the metamorphosis had completed, he now found himself standing at his father's cremation. Except for the vicar and the pallbearers, there was no one else in attendance at the funeral at all.

Alan now watched silently as the cheap coffin started moving along the metallic conveyor, and the burgundy curtains opened to allow it to pass through, and then they closed behind it. He heard the roar of the flames from behind the curtains. His father's body was turned to ash, and those ashes had been buried in an unmarked grave that no one would ever visit. Alan had never even asked where they were buried.

He had no idea that he would ever regret the way that he had turned his back on his father. Now he felt a huge sense of loss and failure on his part. His father may have failed him, but he had also failed his father. He knew deep down that if he had tried, then maybe he could have helped him. He had never even tried though, and this was the whole point of him seeing this. The room shifted around him again. Now all that was left was just the table with a half-drunk bottle of whiskey on top of it and an empty chair.

He now felt that he could leave the room having learnt the lesson that he was here to be taught. He started walking towards the door when he spotted a black and white picture lying on the floor. He stopped and bent down to pick it up. It was a picture of his father, and it had been taken. He was a young child. He was sat with his back against a brick wall in a playground somewhere, and he was all alone.

He had been alone for most of his life. The look of sadness and loneliness was etched on his face even back then. The picture made Alan sad. He had never seen it before. His hand started to shake again as his emotions began to well up inside of him. He needed to let go of the pain. He dropped the picture to the floor. By the time it had landed, the picture had already faded away to nothing. He closed the door behind him as he left his father's life and death behind the door.

There was only one more room left for him to explore. During the last few hours, he had been humbled and saddened in ways that he had never expected. He had been reminded of his inhumanity and his lack of grace throughout all of his life. Every choice that he had made had consequences, and only now did he fully understand the full effects of those choices and the way that he had chosen to live his life.

He walked up to the final door without any hesitation. He immediately placed the key in the lock, and he unlocked the door. He stood as tall as he could as he walked on into the room. He was already broken. There was nothing more left that could hurt him any deeper. Or so he thought. He could never have been ready for what he found inside of that final room.

He walked through the door, and he found that he was in the boardroom of his company. There was an empty seat at the table that belonged to him, and he walked over to take his place at the head of the table.

Alison Faith was the head of the human resource department. She was about to begin her presentation that would see ten of his staff being made redundant. It was a cost-cutting exercise that he had ordered, despite the company making record-breaking profits the previous year. He wanted to get even more out of his staff.

He listened to the presentation, and then he gave his permission for the cuts in the staffing levels to go ahead. It was just as he had done three years earlier. There were further cuts that he could make, and they would happen in time. This was a business decision, and he wasn't ashamed of it at all. He had nothing to feel guilty about here.

There was a period of consultation for all of those who were going to be affected. There were interviews conducted, and the tough decisions were taken. They assured the staff affected that those decisions were not taken lightly and that the redundancies were necessary to make the company ready to face an uncertain future in an increasingly competitive industry. In reality, the choices had already been made before the consultations had even started.

Alan was the one who would be left to tell the staff. He would hand out the letters telling the staff that unfortunately, they were the ones who had been chosen to lose their jobs. He was sure that they would all find something else soon, and that was just what he had told them all. In all honesty, he didn't care. They were no longer his problem once they were gone.

Jay Dart was the last man to be told, and this was where Alan now found himself again. He handed Jay the letter personally, and Jay looked devastated as he had read it. It was confusing to Alan. Why would he see this again? Out of the ten people he had let go, why was he now seeing only Jay?

He had remembered the meeting well. He watched himself handing Jay the letter, and Jay pleading with him not to choose him. He had a nine-year-old son, a seven-year-old daughter and his wife had twins on the way. He was dedicated to his family, and all he wanted to do was to provide for them.

Alan had offered Jay his sympathy, but he could offer him nothing else along with it. He could not keep him on, not even in a part-time position. The decision had been made by the higher powers, and there was nothing he could do about it. That was what he told Jay anyway. Of course, it was all a complete lie, but Jay would never find that out. This was all down to Alan and Alan alone.

Jay was chosen purely because of the time he had been with the company, and also because he had young children with more on the way. He was a good worker, but he would not have to be paid a redundancy payout due to his short length of service. His wife and children seemed to be sick a lot of the time too. That meant Jay was taking time off to help care for them.

Of course, that could never be said officially, but to Alan, it had helped him to make up his mind. With another two children on the way, the time that he spent away from the company was likely to get even worse. They couldn't keep being down on staff numbers. It had all stacked up against him. Jay was devastated. There were very few jobs in the area, and he was just about getting by as it was. The decision had already been made though, and that was that.

Time moved quickly forwards, and the room evolved around him again. Now he found himself somewhere that he did not recognise. He was in Jay's house, and it was the families dinner time. The children were eating cold value supermarket spaghetti on plain bread. Alan could feel that it was very cold in the house. The lights were turned off, and so was the television.

Jay and his wife were sat at the table with the children. Neither of them had anything on the table to eat in front of them. Jay had been unable to find a job since being made redundant, and when his wife had suffered severe stomach pains, he had missed an appointment at the jobcentre. The family had been sanctioned for his non-attendance, and they were currently receiving no money at all apart from the child benefit. They were relying on charity gifts and parcels from the food banks just to survive.

"You need to eat something for the babies," Jay said to his wife.

"I ate something earlier. I'm feeling a little sick now." She lied. The emergency electric that was left on the key meter had run out. Jay had no idea where he was going to get any more money from now. He felt such a failure.

Later that night, he would go out and steal food for his family from the supermarket. He felt that he had no other choice left open to him. He had to feed his family. Eventually, he would be caught and fined by the court for shoplifting. It was a fine that he could not afford to pay either.

The room then began to shift forward in time again. Alan now found himself standing in a classroom. Alan started walking between the rows of desks. He noticed that Jay's son Nicholas was sitting at one of the desks in front of him. He looked pale. He wasn't getting enough nutrients in his body. That was plain for anyone to see. The teacher then made an excuse and stepped out of the classroom for a moment. Nicholas now looked terrified. He already knew what was going to happen now that the teacher had gone.

Two of the other boys in the class got up from their chairs. They came straight over to where Nicholas was sitting. He was working away quietly by himself. They then began to taunt him mercilessly.

"Your family are poor!" One of them shouted at

him.

"No, they aren't!" Nicholas shouted back at him, angrily. He knew that it was the truth, but he was ashamed that the whole class was now hearing what was being said. Then the other boy joined in with more taunts.

"Your clothes don't even fit you properly. You're a charity shop beggar!" He shouted. The rest of the class all now started laughing at Nicholas. Only one girl stood up to defend him. Her name was Anne.

"Leave him alone!" She protested. Nicholas was grateful, but he was also upset that he could not stand up to the bullies himself without fear of him being beaten up. He was scared of the bullies. They knew it, and they fed on his fears, and it encouraged them even more.

The bullies stopped taunting him for a second, and then one of them smiled at the other. He then started chanting.

"Anne fancies Nick, Anne fancies Nick..." He repeated the ditty over and over again.

"No, she doesn't!" Nick shouted back, angrily. He jumped up in his chair, and then he felt a blow strike him on the top of his head.

One of the boys had punched him on the head, and now he felt dizzy with pain. He tried his hardest not to cry, but he could not stop himself no matter what he did. This had been going on since his Dad had lost his job. He couldn't take any more of it. Then the boys started with another taunt.

"Crybaby, crybaby, crybaby, crybaby!" It seemed as if the whole class was now singing along with them. Alan was feeling sick at what he was seeing and hearing.

He had never thought for one second that his actions might have caused this amount of suffering to Jay’s young son.

"Leave him be! This is not his fault. It’s mine!"

Alan shouted out, but the children could not see or hear him.

Nicholas jumped up from his chair, and then he started running towards the door. He could not take any more of this torture. One of the boys tripped him as he started to run. He fell forwards, and he slid right across the floor. As he slid, he felt his trousers ripping wide open at the groin.

His trousers now had a massive hole in them, and he could not hide his shame. His mother would not be able to sew them up and repair them. This was his only pair of school trousers, and now they were ruined. Almost everyone was now laughing at him yet again.

He jumped up with fresh tears in his eyes, and he ran straight out of the classroom door. He was going home. He ran all the way there, sobbing as he did. The bedroom evolved a further time around Alan, who could only wait helplessly to see what the outcome of all of this was.

Now they were back at Nick's parent's home again. The back door to the house was open as it always was, and Nicholas had let himself inside. Jay was out looking for work, and his mother was asleep on the sofa with a duvet wrapped around her to keep her warm. Nicholas walked into the living room and kissed his mother on the forehead while she slept.

"I love you, mum." He said. Then he started sobbing all over again. He walked out of the front room, and he headed for the stairs. Alan now found himself standing up in the child's bedroom. He could not believe what was unravelling in front of his eyes.

Nicholas had run into the room, and he had continued sobbing as he tore a piece of paper from his school book. He then started writing out a handwritten note to his family. He had then taken the belt off from his trousers. He placed the note on the side where it would be found. Alan walked across the room to read it. It said:

Sorry Mum and Dad, but I ripped my trousers, and I know you have no money to buy me new ones. I don't want you to worry because of me. I love you both. Kiss Sammy goodbye for me.xxx

Samantha was his little sister. Alan could not fully understand what was happening. Surely this could not have happened? The boy was still a child, and he was being tortured for the decision that Alan had made. It was his choice. He had been the cause of all this pain. That poor child had suffered relentlessly because of his decision. He shook his head, and as he turned back around, Nicholas was already hanging by his neck from the top tier of his bunk bed.

The child's lips were now blue. His eyes were wide in his head, and his tongue was hanging out loosely from his mouth.

"NO, NO, NO!" Alan screamed out loud. He ran over to the child, and he tried to lift him to support his weight. His hands just slipped right through the child’s body. Alan couldn't save him.

He wasn't here in the room when it had happened, and the child was already long dead.

Sammy was now running up the stairs, and she entered the bedroom that she shared with her older brother. She had heard that he was being picked on at school again, and she wanted to make sure that he was alright. She burst into the room, and she could not comprehend what she saw in front of her. She dropped her school bag down on the floor, and she let out an inhuman scream of pain that came straight from her heart.

"Get him some help!" Alan shouted, but Sammy could not hear him, she was screaming louder and louder, and on hearing her daughter’s cries, her mother started climbing up the stairs as quickly as she could.

When her mother opened up the bedroom door, she ran over to her son, and she lifted him in the air. She couldn't undo the belt and lift him at the same time. She was crying out frantically for help. Sammy was the one who had to help her undo the belt that was wrapped tightly around her brother's neck. They were both too late to save him.

Alan walked backwards until he could go no further. He was pressed up against the bedroom wall, and this place would not let him leave without him seeing the end of this. His face was full of shame, but there was even more pain yet still to come. The child's mother was sat down on the floor with her cold dead son resting on her lap. She was stroking his soft hair and rocking him backwards and forwards while she cried.

He was her flesh and blood, she had once given him life, and she had to try and bring him back to her. Then the blood started to pool between her legs as the shock of what was happening caused her to miscarry both of her twins. Alan had to turn his face away. He could not look at this anymore. The room then began to evolve once again.

When Alan turned around, Jay and his wife were sitting in an undertaker's office. Jay looked beaten and defeated, and he looked like he was ready to give up on life. His wife was looking at the pictures of the children's coffins and the prices that were underneath them.

"We can't afford any of these." She said. Then she repeated herself over and over again while she rocked backwards and forwards in her chair.

The room then changed around him for one final time. Alan was spared the pain of having to see the child's funeral, but he was not spared from the end of the family's story. He now found himself standing in a chapel of rest. Jay, his wife, and Sammy were all now lying in coffins. Their bodies were all now at rest.

There was no explanation as to why or how they had died, but they were all gone. Alan had heard that Jay had gone off the rails, but no one had told him any of the details. No one had told him about his family, either. He had never even called him to see if he was alright.

It was Jay's wife that had a fatal accident. She had become severely depressed after losing three of her children and placed on high dosage anti-depressants and sleeping tablets. She was walking around like a zombie most of the time. One morning while she was trying to make breakfast, she had put some eggs in the large saucepan along with some water then she had turned on the gas in the kitchen without lighting the ignition properly. Then she had sat down on the sofa while she waited for the water to boil.

She had then fallen asleep, and she had dreamt a pleasant dream about her firstborn son. The windows in the house had been sealed up with plastic sheeting to try and keep the drafts out. They had even covered up the air vents trying to keep the house warm. The gas soon spread throughout the house, killing them all where they slept. They would all be together as a family again.

His choices had caused the death of an entire family. There was nothing he could do to make that right. There was nothing he could do to change what he had done. He was guilty, and he would take full responsibility for what he did. This was down to no one else but him. He was worthless, heartless and spineless. He was a fraud, and he had failed them all.

The room slowly began to shift back to the boardroom that he had first entered. The table was now empty. He finally realised that the choices made in this room had far more reaching consequences than he could have ever imagined. When he got back home, he was going to start treating his staff a lot better. He owed them that at least.

He saw the door appear, and he walked over to it. He had survived the lessons from all five of the rooms, but it had come at a massive cost. He opened the door, and then he turned around to look back into the room. Now it was back to being a bedroom again, with the same standard decoration that was in the first two rooms. It had that same standard furniture inside of it as well. He never wanted to see another room like this in his life. He closed the door tightly shut behind him, and then he locked it to seal it away.

In the hallway, the lights now seemed to burn much brighter than when he had first entered the landing. From the stairwell, he could see what he thought was daylight now coming from downstairs. It looked like he had managed to survive the night after all. Now he would have to try and make amends, or at least he would do what was right from now on.

He walked along the whole length of the hallway towards the stairs, and as he passed by each bedroom door, they each faded away into the wall. He did not look back, not even once. He did not see that the walls were turning pure white behind him either.

The place was cleansing itself in preparation for the next visitor who was to come here. Some of the visitors would have more doors to enter, some would have less, but all of the doors would have to be opened if the visitor ever wanted to leave this place again.

As he began to descend the stairs, he was glad that there no more rooms left for him to explore. He had been mentally battered and bruised for the entire night, and it had left him a broken man. He couldn't take any more of this even if he wanted to. He then noticed movement at the bottom of the stairs. There was someone else here in the guest house with him.

"Hey!" He shouted out. The figure at the bottom of the stairs looked up at him and smiled, and then the figure moved behind the reception desk and out of sight of Alan's line of vision.

The figure he had just seen was that of a portly older man. What was left of his thinning hair was grey, and he wore small circular spectacles that were perched on the bridge of his nose. His trousers seemed to be pulled up far too far above his waist, and the shirt that he wore looked to be an off white colour as if it had been through a few washes along with other darker mixed colours. Alan almost jumped down the last few stairs. He was hoping that the figure was real and not just another figment of his imagination like the butler from the previous night.

As he reached the bottom stair, he could see that the older man was still there. He was standing behind the reception desk, and he was writing away furiously. His handwriting matched the writing that was on the master key fob.

"Thank God that you are real," Alan said. The man then put his hand up in front of his face, as if he were asking Alan to wait for a few seconds. Then after a short pause, he eventually spoke.

"Bear with me. I am just writing out the last one." He said. Alan felt a huge sense of relief. Now he could get out of here. He could get back to his own home at last. He needed a good sleep, the comfort of his luxurious bed, and he fully intended to sleep for the rest of the day.

As he waited for the man to finish writing, Alan noticed that something was different. He was looking over at the bookshelf. Each of the books now had something written on the outside of them. He walked over to take a closer look at them, and each of the books now had dates and numbers perfectly written on the outside of every single one. The last one of the books was missing.

"It's almost over now." The older man told him. He was still busily writing away behind the desk. "There is just one more thing before we start the next volume." He said. The man seemed a little odd. If he had been the person who had filled in all of the books by himself, then he must have been writing them all night. Even then, it would have been an impressive feat if they were all fully completed.

The man behind the counter then dropped his pen down on the desk.

"I don't know how this one ends." He said. Then

he stared at Alan, looking genuinely confused. "Forgive me. I get so caught up in my work, that I forget myself sometimes." He was now smiling.

"Do you have a phone that I can use? My car broke down, and I need to make a call." Alan pleaded with him. The man just looked at him for a second, and then he started laughing at him under his breath.

"No, haha. No phones work in here I'm afraid. All we sometimes get is a little static." He replied. He had found the question highly amusing.

"Then is there someone local who can fix my car for me?" He asked. The man was smiling at him again, and it was becoming rather irritating. After the night that he had just experienced, he didn't need any further delays.

"There is nothing else here. There is no one else here at present either. This is between you and me alone." The man was now no longer smiling at him or laughing anymore.

“What is this place, and who are you?” Alan demanded to know.

“This is the halfway house, and I am the Architect.” He replied. The man was talking in riddles. Alan’s patience with the man was wearing thin. He wasn't going to listen to much more of this nonsense before he finally snapped.

“I asked you what this place was, not what it was called.” He said, and his tone was becoming sharper.

The man took off his glasses and folded them closed. Then he placed them down carefully on the desk. This wasn't the first time that he had been over this conversation, and everyone who came through here reacted to the experience in a different way. The man took in a deep breath before he began to explain. Then he was ready to tell Alan what he needed to know.

“This is the place that exists between life and death. This is where the story of your life is reviewed and where your life flashes before your eyes. This is where you see those that you loved again for one last time. Your place to remember and regret." He said. His voice sounded soothing and relaxed. It was almost like he was reading from a well-rehearsed speech.

Now it was Alan's turn to smile back at the man.

"Take a look for yourself." The man said, and he pointed in the direction of the bookcase. Alan stormed over to the books, and he snatched the very first one out from the shelf. He opened up the pages, and each one was perfectly written out by hand, without a single mistake anywhere. He flipped through the pages and seeing that they were all filled in, he turned back to the very start of the book.

There it was in his hands in front of him. It was written out by hand in black ink. The date, time, minute and second that he had taken his very first breath. What was written on the following pages was an expertly catalogued description of every single event that had ever occurred throughout all of his entire life. Nothing had been missed out. Every single thing that he ever did, every emotion that he ever felt, and every other person that he had interacted with in his life, they were all written down in the book.

His face dropped, and he placed the book back in its place on the shelf. Then he turned around to face the man behind the desk, and the colour had all drained away from Alan's face.

"Ah, the moment of realisation finally dawns. Don't worry. You are not the first person to be as afraid as you are right now." He was right, Alan was afraid.

Alan was not just afraid, he was bemused and ashamed in equal measure. He had been the one narrating his own life story during the night. His memories had fed the rooms. His five greatest mistakes and regrets of his life had played out like miniature movies for him to relive all over again.

Alan wondered if this was what it felt like to drown. To have your lungs fill up with water and to fight against the need to breathe while the water flooded into your lungs and filled up every single pocket with fluid.

"So, what happens now?" Alan asked. He was now feeling very uncertain. He had never believed in the concept of a heaven or hell or any afterlife. Yet here he stood, looking over the edge of a precipice and into the unknown when he expected to find nothing but eternal darkness.

The man looked at him straight in the eye. It was the first time that Alan had looked into his eyes closely. Inside of his pupils there seemed to be an eternal void that seemed to stretch back to the edge of forever.

"I don't know how the story ends." The man said. "I didn't write it though, you did. Now, all that I can see is the good and the bad in your life, and it is clear that the bad outweighs the good. I just have to decide if there is enough reason to enter a plea on your behalf. I can see no reason for me to interfere, so the next decision must be yours and yours alone."

The man then waved his hand from side to side in front of him, and the wall behind Alan started shifting in shape. There were now three doors in the wall that was directly behind him.

"You now have three choices open to you, Alan. The door on the left leads you back outside. If you choose this door, you will face the wolf waiting outside of the door. He will be the one who decides your fate for you, but he is not known for his compassion.

The middle door leads to salvation, but only those deemed worthy may pass on through it. The door on the right leads to eternal damnation and suffering, as you descend through the seven levels of hell, and finally, you will fall deep down into the inferno below."

He painted the pictures so beautifully that Alan felt that he was spoilt for choice. He could either face the wolf that was waiting outside of the door and risk being torn to shreds by the animal. Or he could make a choice for himself. The choice was eternal damnation and pain, or did he think that he was worthy of salvation?

"How long do I have?" Alan asked.

The Architect then pulled up an hourglass filled with sand out from underneath the counter. He turned it upside down, and the sand began to flow. It would be empty in a very short space of time.

"When the sands of time run clear, the wolf will come for you, and the doors will all disappear. Choose wisely, my friend." He said. Then he turned around and walked back into the office behind the reception. He then closed the door behind him. The stairs had now disappeared along with the fireplace and the dining-room door.

This is the end

The sands of time within the hourglass were ebbing away quickly. Alan stood in the middle of the reception room facing all three of the doors. The left-hand door seemed the easiest option to choose, but he feared the pain of being torn to shreds by the wolf that was waiting outside for him. The middle door led to salvation, but he was unsure if he deserved salvation. He then looked at the door on the right. It felt foreboding and scary, just to even look at it.

The thoughts of the previous night flashed through his head again. He thought about the memories of his mother and father, then of Atlanta, his unborn daughter, and of the families whose lives he had ruined. He thought of the child who was hanging from the bed and of all of his other unexplored regrets. Yes, he regretted every single bad thing that had happened in his life. He finally, truly understood that no one else had made those choices, and he had carried the repercussions of those choices silently with him throughout all of his life. Yet he felt that regretting his actions was not enough to save him from what he had done.

He took the letter opener out of his pocket, and he held it out in front of him. He then braced himself, and he ran forward. He ran straight through the door on the right that would lead him to eternal damnation. He hated himself for all of the pain that he had caused to others. There were many more who were far more worthy of salvation than him.

He deserved whatever fate awaited him on the other side of the door, and now there was no going back as he crashed through the wooden door and down into the darkness beyond.

What are the chances?

The letter opener was no longer in his hand. His clothes had all been removed from his body as well. Now it was just him alone as he was falling. He was naked as he fell endlessly down through the void. He fell further and further down through the darkness. He may have been falling for minutes, or it may have been days. There was no concept of time here.

This was what his vision of death had been all along. An eternity spent in the darkness all alone. There was nothing he could do in here. He could not even make a sound. He could move his arms and legs and head, but he could do nothing else. Then he landed on a soft cushioned surface, and his body started to become covered in a thick fluid, it filled his lungs to the point where he felt that he would choke.

It may well have been petrol in his lungs for all that he knew. He might soon experience the fires of hell that he had never once believed in before, not even for one second. He then started to hear a sound that felt as if it were coming from all around him. It was a dull thud that sounded like a drumbeat repeating over and over again. It was coming from all around him.

The sound that he heard was a heartbeat. He realised that it must have been his heartbeat pounding loudly within the fluid that he was now surrounded in that he was hearing. The liquid had filled up his lungs completely, but he did not drown. Finally, he stopped feeling so afraid. Something was now protecting him from harm. He felt the power of a love that was so strong that it could not be defeated by time. It was a love that he had not felt since he was a child who was being held in his mother's comforting arms.

He opened up his eyes, and now he was moving again. He saw wondrous colours and sights, and then he grew afraid as he saw what appeared to be a giant spider on a wall up ahead of him. It was a sight that he would never forget. Then he saw the light up ahead, and he felt himself being pushed down towards that light. He closed his eyes again in readiness for the pain that was to come, and he felt a crushing sensation as if the life was being squeezed from his body.

The last entry

The office door opened, and the Architect was ready to make his final entry. He walked on over to the reception desk, and he picked up the pen once again. He placed the nib back down on the open page of the book, and he began to write the final lines in the last book.

'Alan finally passed over on the sixteenth of May. During his judgement, he showed genuine signs of remorse, and ultimately he felt unworthy of salvation. He chose to face his punishment for his sins, and he was granted a reprieve. This is his final opportunity to make a difference. He takes a gift along with him. The gift is one of light and a soul of an unborn who would have made the world a better place. She almost passed me by as well." Then he closed the book and walked over to the bookcase. He placed it in the last place on the shelf, and now he would have to prepare for his next visitor.

Alan had never felt pain like this before, and he was dragged out into the light by his head, then he was lifted by his feet. He could not see what was going on around him, but he could make out blurry images of the giant demons that were now surrounding him.

He was so afraid of what was about to happen that he soiled himself. He was now choking on the fluid that had filled his lungs, and he had been ripped away from warmth and protection that he had felt surrounding him.

He felt another pain like he had never felt before, and the giants started to cut his lifeline away from him. They had begun to cut away at his body, and then one of them then struck him hard. He cried out in pain at the stinging sensation, and the sudden realisation of what was happening forced his tears.

He had just been born to the world all over again. The recollections of his previous life were gone, erased from his memory. The slate was now clean. She had been given a second chance, along with a gift. Now she had to do this all by herself.

Exit 12, M3, A303, Home

The wreck of the car was not found until the following morning. It had struck a pothole in the road, and one of the tyres had exploded. The damage to the wheel had caused the car to flip over and over again until it landed on the other side of the embankment with the driver still trapped inside.

In this distance, there was a barren tree. It felt oddly out of place, and nothing seemed to grow in the field that it was placed in at all. None of the animals would go anywhere near it. It was clear to the investigating officers that the driver of the car had been speeding recklessly, and at his age, he should have known better. A front wheel blow out after hitting a pothole at the speed that he was travelling at, was only ever going to end one way.

The emergency services had been called to the scene, to try and cut out the driver from the wreckage, but no one held out much hope for him from the moment they had seen the state of the car. The fire crew had eventually cut the body free. The doctor had pronounced Alan Reed dead at the scene.

They would later estimate that Alan Reed had died at around eight-thirty the previous evening. There was no one left in his family to sue for the accident, and the pothole was quickly filled in to prevent any further incidents. The repair to the road was only temporary, and it lasted just a few months before it had started to crumble away again.

Rain

There was something mysterious about the child. She seemed gifted and somehow special. She was clever, kind and generous to everyone that she met. She loved to play with dolls and to make new friends. Anyone who had ever encountered her would say that she never had a bad bone in her body.

Whenever it rained, it would bring a smile to her face. She would often sit in her bedroom and watch the rain falling outside of her window. No one else could see them, but she could see them every single time. As the rain would flow down her window, she would be staring out and far beyond the pane of glass, and she would watch in wonder as the fireflies danced a magical dance in the rain.

Her parents had named her Atlanta Rain. They had no idea where the idea for the name had come from though. It just seemed to fit with her character perfectly.

At six years old, Atlanta awoke from a dream with a vivid recollection. There was an old house out in a village, and there were five doors upstairs that had hidden secrets kept inside. The house was in a village called Grimfall, where a kind older man and an evil wolf had battled with each other constantly across time. The final battle was about to begin.

Her parents checked every map of the country, even ones online that were hundreds of years old, but the village of Grimfall could not be found anywhere on any one of them.

Printed in Great Britain
by Amazon

74649348R00118